TAO

The Little Samurai

pranks #1
and Attacks!

Laurent Richard
illustrated by **Nicolas Ryser**
Translation: **Edward Gavin**

GRAPHIC UNIVERSE™ • MINNEAPOLIS

STORY BY LAURENT RICHARD
ILLUSTRATIONS BY NICOLAS RYSER
TRANSLATION BY EDWARD GAUVIN

FIRST AMERICAN EDITION PUBLISHED IN 2014 BY GRAPHIC UNIVERSE™.

FARCES ET ATTAQUES! BY LAURENT RICHARD AND NICOLAS RYSER © BAYARD ÉDITIONS, 2011
COPYRIGHT © 2014 BY LERNER PUBLISHING GROUP, INC., FOR THE US EDITION

GRAPHIC UNIVERSE™ IS A TRADEMARK OF LERNER PUBLISHING GROUP, INC.

GRAPHIC UNIVERSE™
A DIVISION OF LERNER PUBLISHING GROUP, INC.
241 FIRST AVENUE NORTH
MINNEAPOLIS, MN 55401 USA

FOR READING LEVELS AND MORE INFORMATION,
LOOK UP THIS TITLE AT WWW.LERNERBOOKS.COM.

MAIN BODY TEXT SET IN CCWILDWORDS 8.5/10.5.
TYPEFACE PROVIDED BY FONTOGRAPHER.

LIBRARY OF CONGRESS CATALOGING-IN-PUBLICATION DATA

RICHARD, LAURENT, 1968–
    [FARCES ET ATTAQUES! ENGLISH.]
    PRANKS AND ATTACKS! / LAURENT RICHARD ; ILLUSTRATED BY NICOLAS RYSER ; TRANSLATION,
EDWARD GAUVIN. — FIRST AMERICAN EDITION.
        P.   CM. – (TAO, THE LITTLE SAMURAI ; #1)
    SUMMARY: TAO IS A STUDENT AT MASTER SNOW'S MARTIAL ARTS SCHOOL. WITH HIS FRIENDS
RAY AND LEE AND HIS NOT-GIRLFRIEND KAT, HE TRIES TO FOLLOW THE TEACHINGS OF MARTIAL ARTS
MASTERS—OR, MORE OFTEN, FINDS A WAY AROUND THE MASTERS' ADVICE.
    ISBN 978-1-4677-2095-3 (LIB. BDG. : ALK. PAPER)
    ISBN 978-1-4677-2554-5 (EBOOK)
    1. GRAPHIC NOVELS. [1. GRAPHIC NOVELS. 2. MARTIAL ARTS–FICTION. 3. SAMURAI–FICTION.
4. SCHOOLS–FICTION. 5. BEHAVIOR–FICTION.] I. RYSER, NICOLAS, ILLUSTRATOR. II. GAUVIN,
EDWARD, TRANSLATOR. III. TITLE.
PZ7.7.RSPR 2014
741.5'944–DC23   2013027733

MANUFACTURED IN THE UNITED STATES OF AMERICA
1 – VI – 12/31/13

No Point Running Just to Be On Time

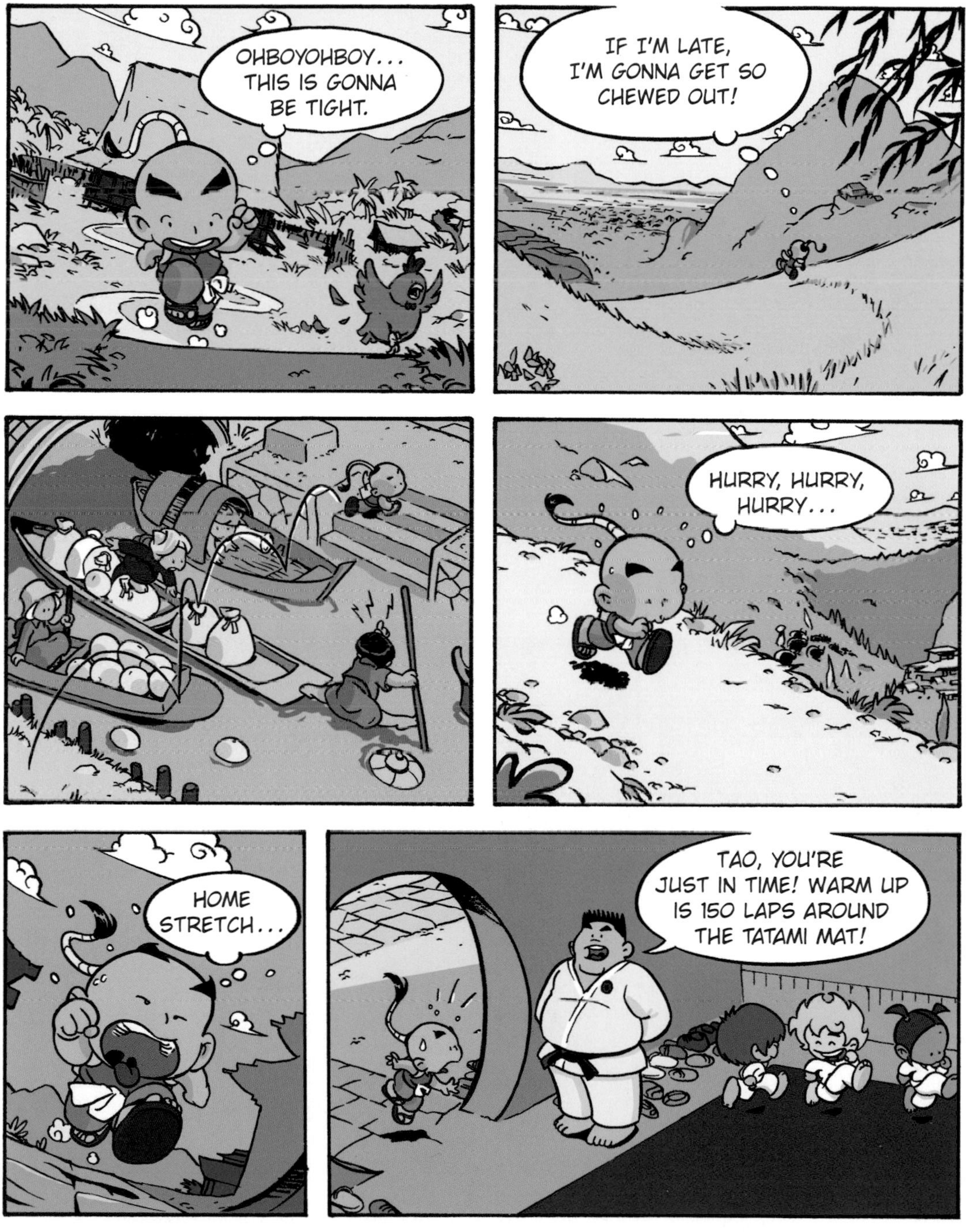
OHBOYOHBOY... THIS IS GONNA BE TIGHT.
IF I'M LATE, I'M GONNA GET SO CHEWED OUT!
HURRY, HURRY, HURRY...
HOME STRETCH...
TAO, YOU'RE JUST IN TIME! WARM UP IS 150 LAPS AROUND THE TATAMI MAT!

Showing Off Can Spoil Dessert

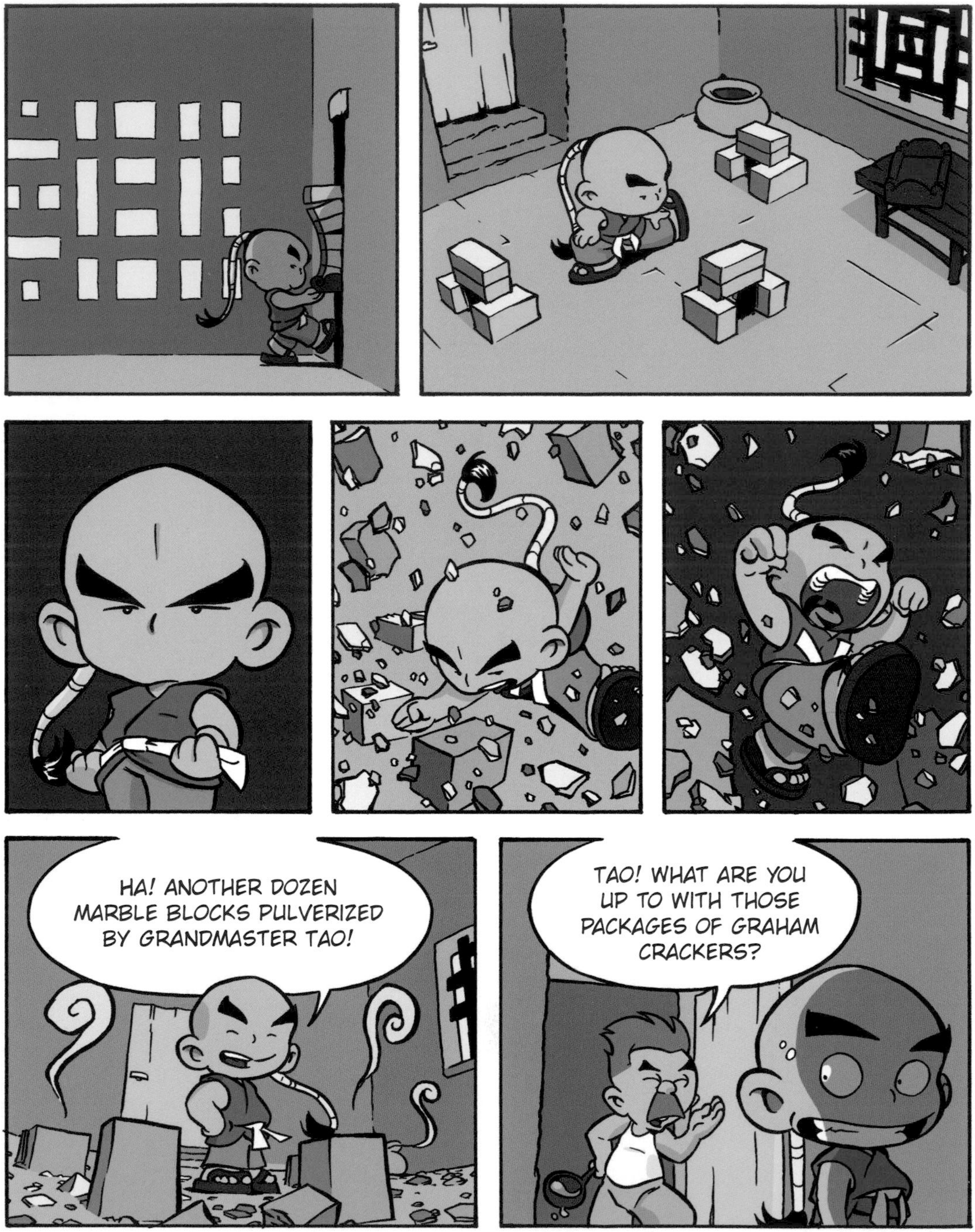
HA! ANOTHER DOZEN MARBLE BLOCKS PULVERIZED BY GRANDMASTER TAO!
TAO! WHAT ARE YOU UP TO WITH THOSE PACKAGES OF GRAHAM CRACKERS?

Clothes Don't Make the Samurai

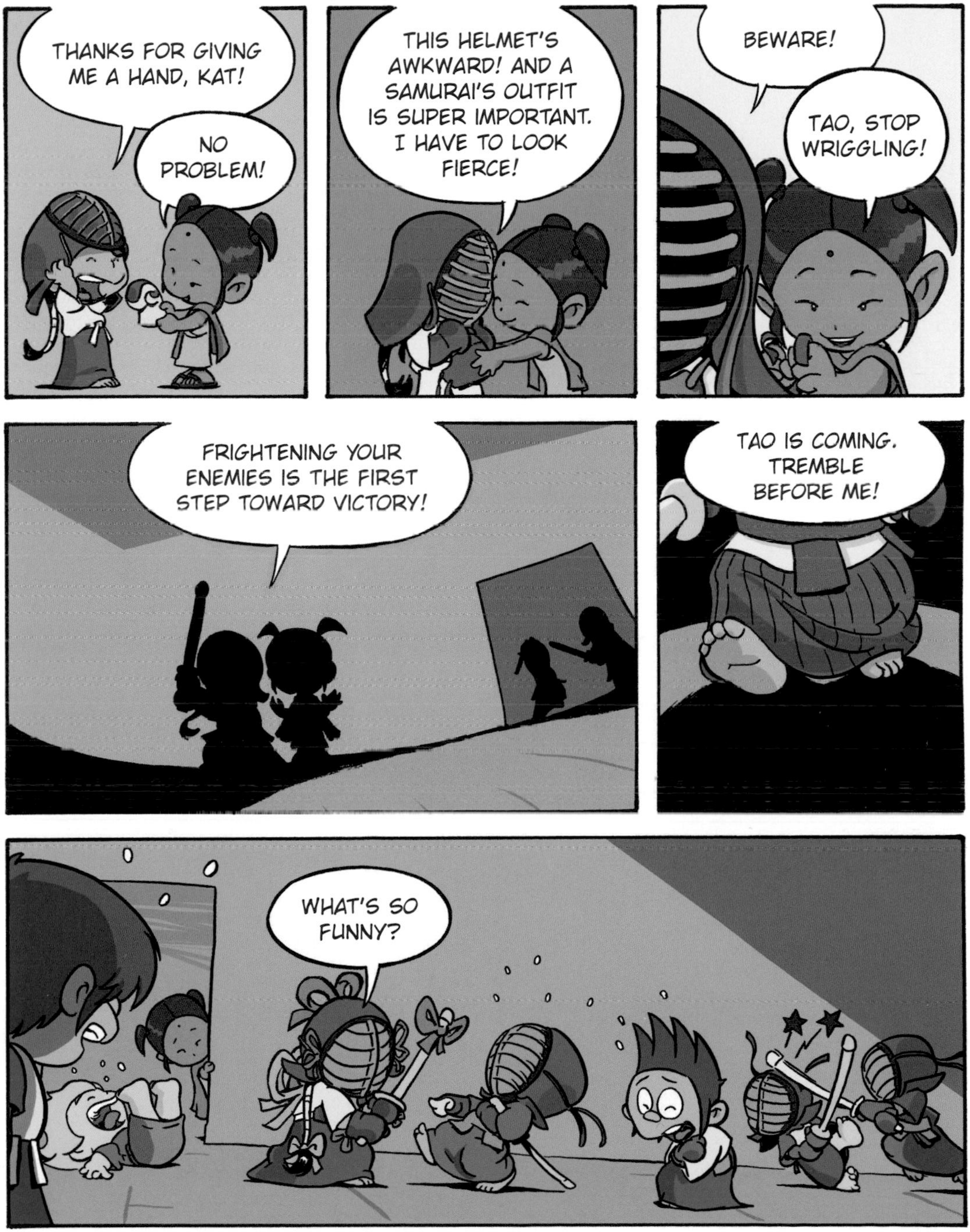
THANKS FOR GIVING ME A HAND, KAT!
NO PROBLEM!
THIS HELMET'S AWKWARD! AND A SAMURAI'S OUTFIT IS SUPER IMPORTANT. I HAVE TO LOOK FIERCE!
BEWARE!
TAO, STOP WRIGGLING!
FRIGHTENING YOUR ENEMIES IS THE FIRST STEP TOWARD VICTORY!
TAO IS COMING. TREMBLE BEFORE ME!
WHAT'S SO FUNNY?

The Grasshopper's Cry Does Not Frighten the Lion

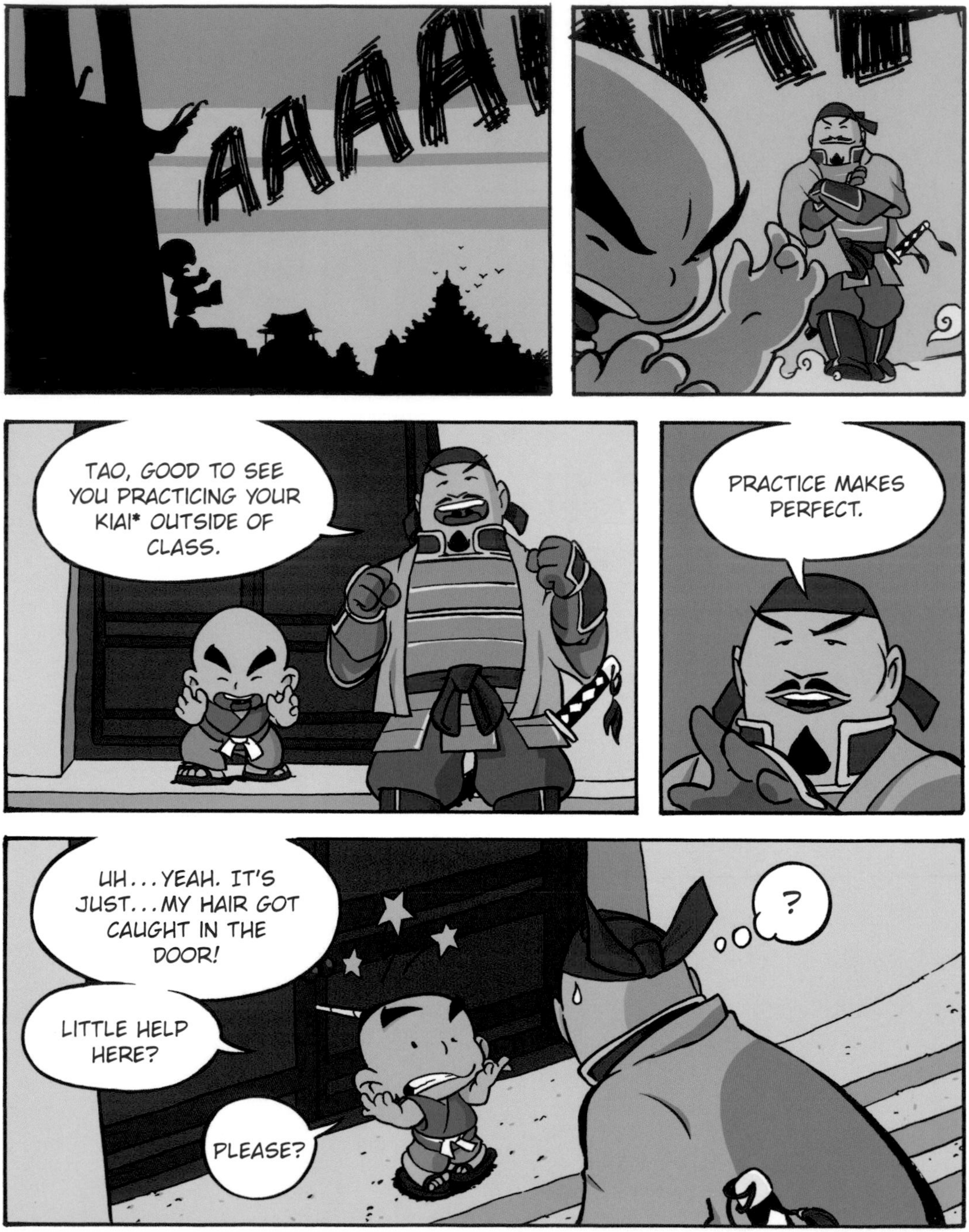
TAO, GOOD TO SEE YOU PRACTICING YOUR KIAI* OUTSIDE OF CLASS.
PRACTICE MAKES PERFECT.
UH...YEAH. IT'S JUST...MY HAIR GOT CAUGHT IN THE DOOR!
LITTLE HELP HERE?
PLEASE?
?

*KIAI: A SHORT YELL MADE BY MARTIAL ARTISTS BEFORE, DURING, OR AFTER A TECHNIQUE

Knot as Easy as It Looks

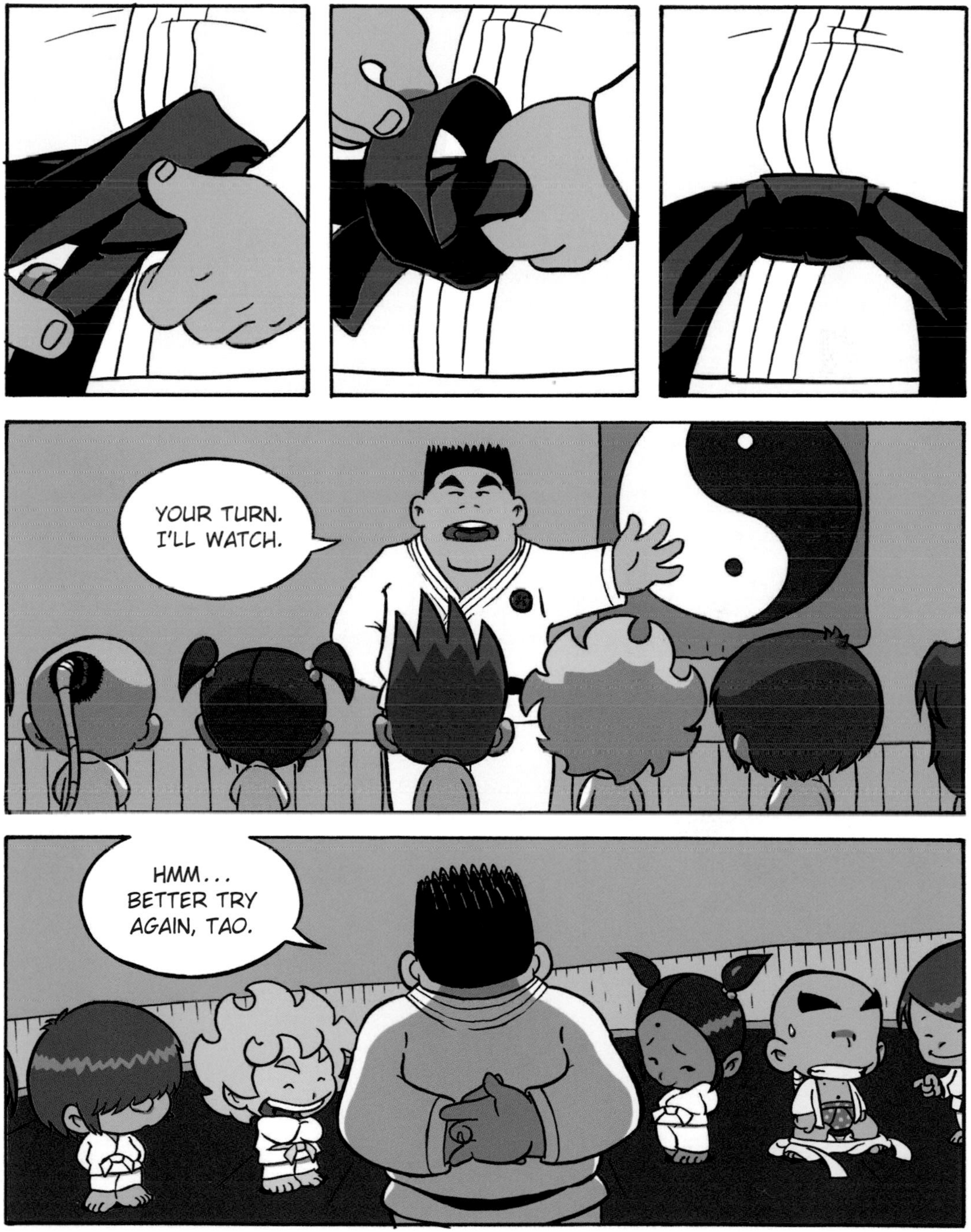
YOUR TURN. I'LL WATCH.
HMM... BETTER TRY AGAIN, TAO.

He Who Would See Far Must First Rise High

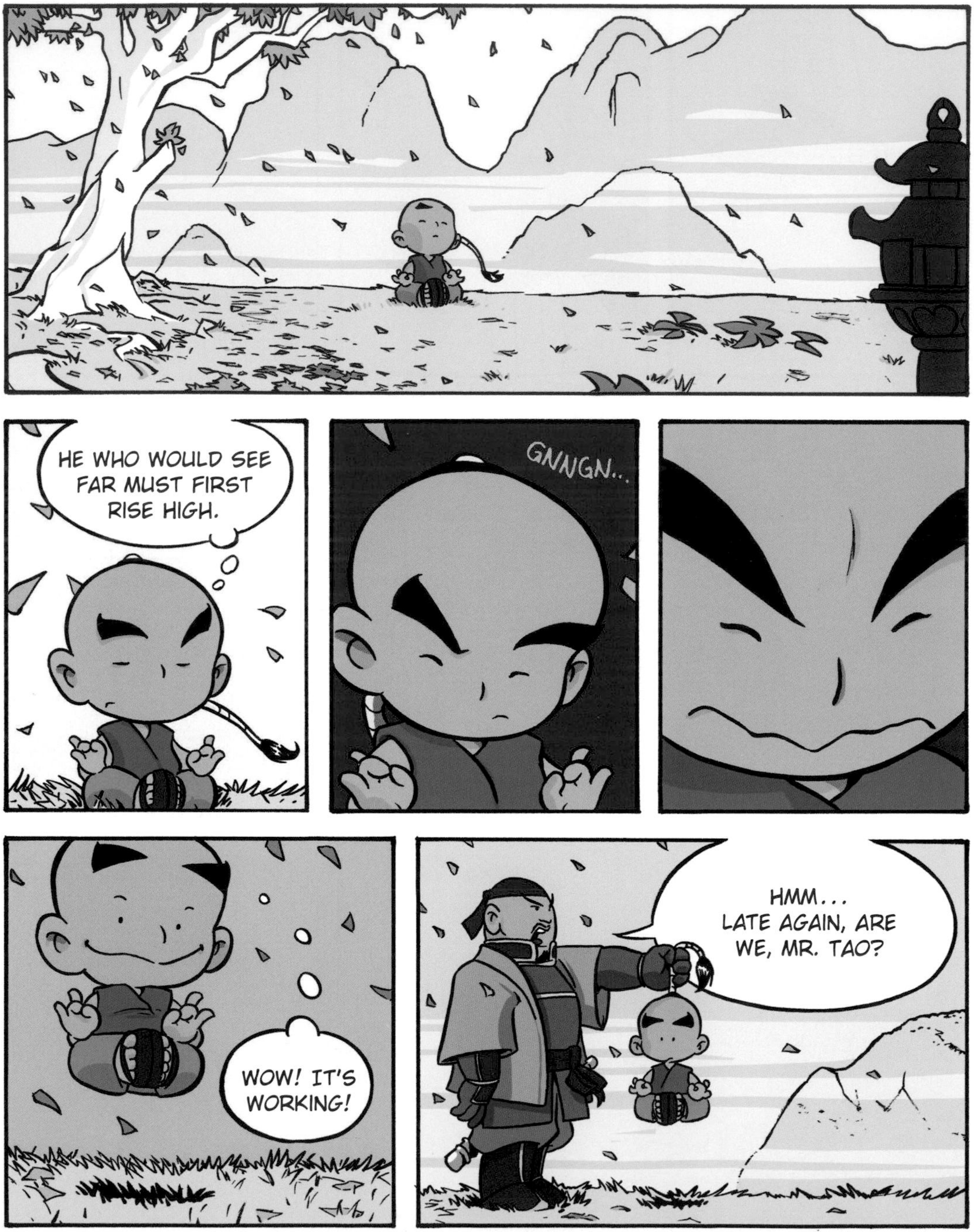

HE WHO WOULD SEE FAR MUST FIRST RISE HIGH.
GNNGN...
WOW! IT'S WORKING!
HMM... LATE AGAIN, ARE WE, MR. TAO?

The Master Shines, the Student Monkeyshines

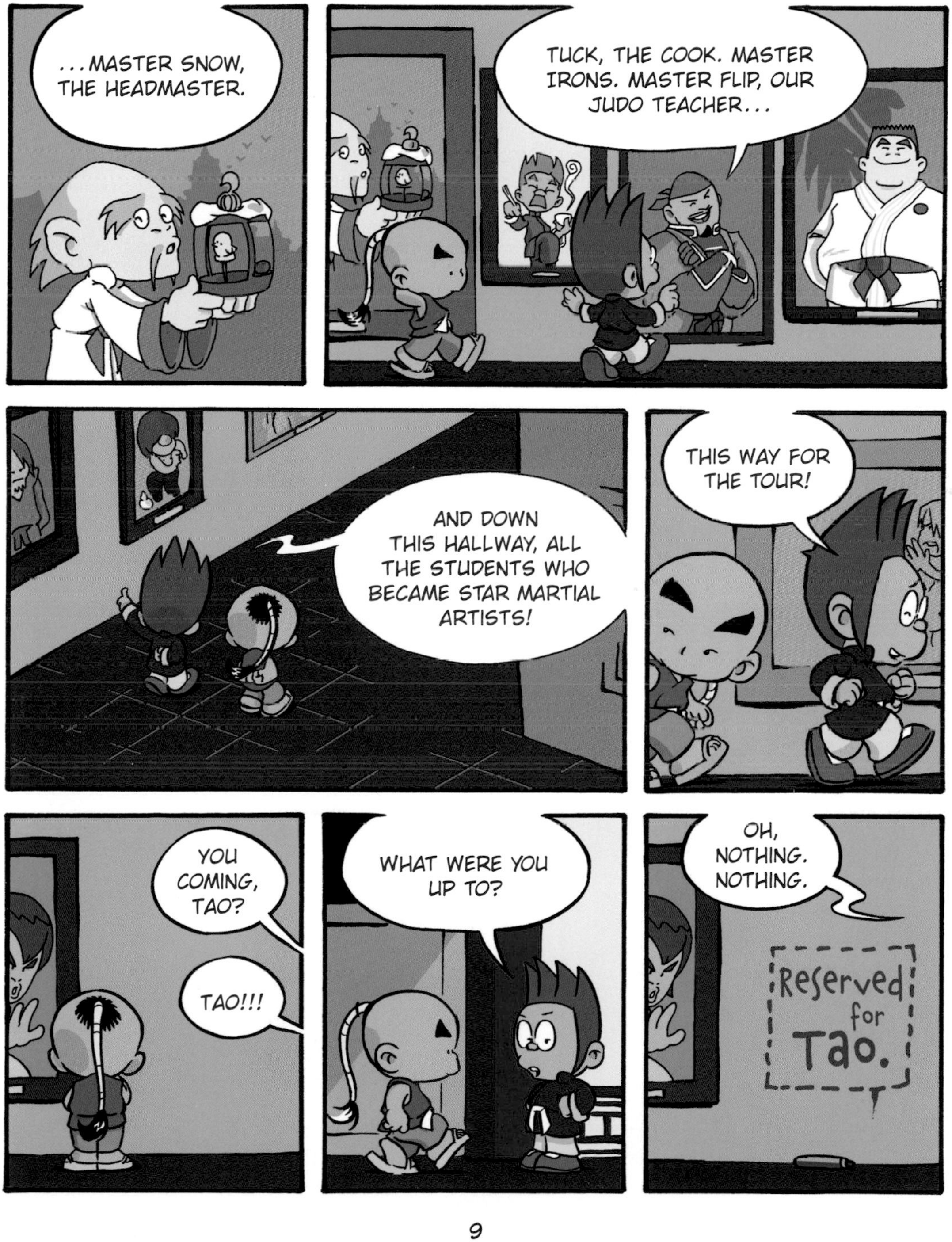
. . . MASTER SNOW, THE HEADMASTER.
TUCK, THE COOK. MASTER IRONS. MASTER FLIP, OUR JUDO TEACHER . . .
AND DOWN THIS HALLWAY, ALL THE STUDENTS WHO BECAME STAR MARTIAL ARTISTS!
THIS WAY FOR THE TOUR!
YOU COMING, TAO?
TAO!!!
WHAT WERE YOU UP TO?
OH, NOTHING. NOTHING.
Reserved for Tao.

He Who Climbs Too Fast Falls Flat on His Face

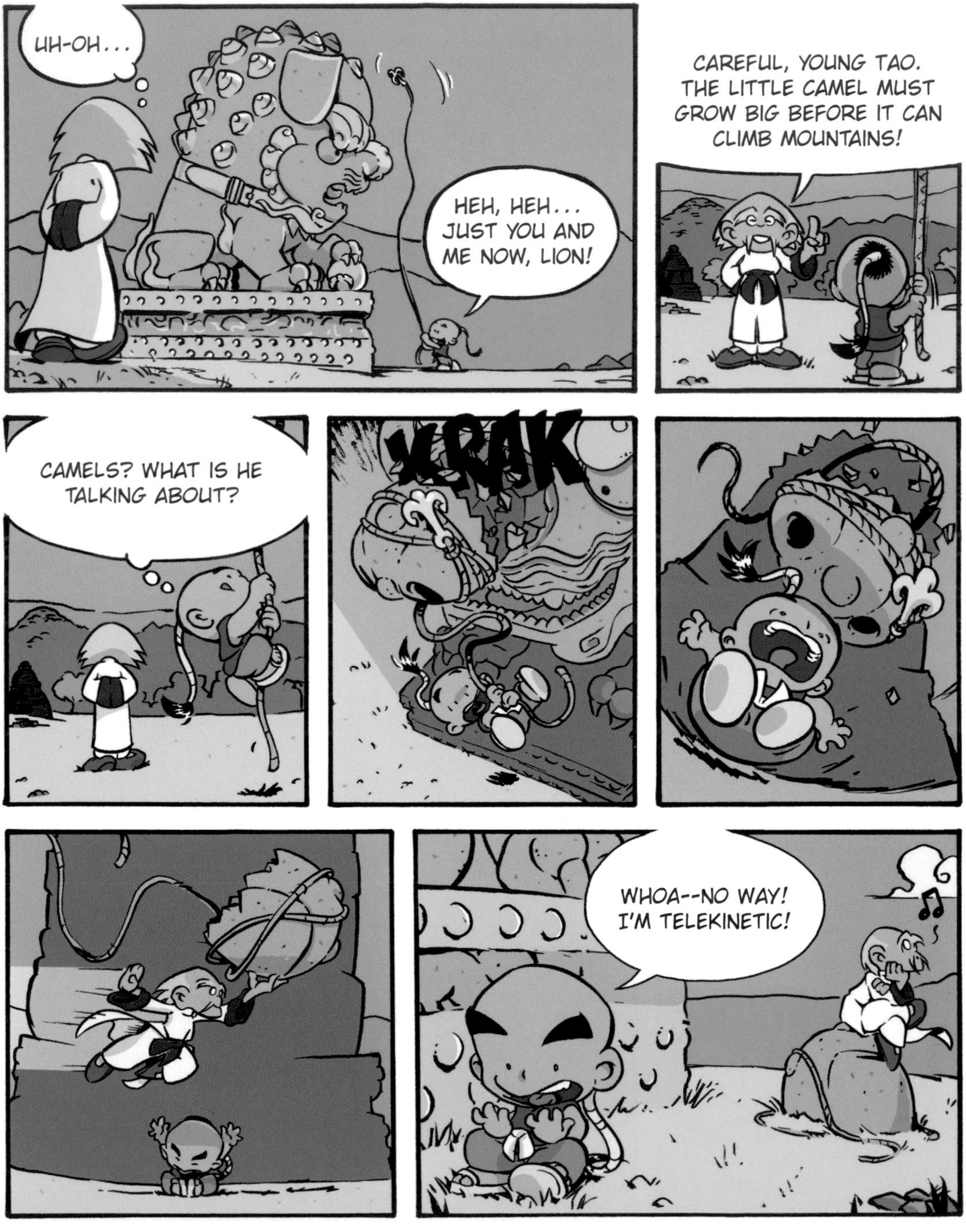
UH-OH . . .
HEH, HEH . . . JUST YOU AND ME NOW, LION!
CAREFUL, YOUNG TAO. THE LITTLE CAMEL MUST GROW BIG BEFORE IT CAN CLIMB MOUNTAINS!
CAMELS? WHAT IS HE TALKING ABOUT?
KRAK
WHOA--NO WAY! I'M TELEKINETIC!

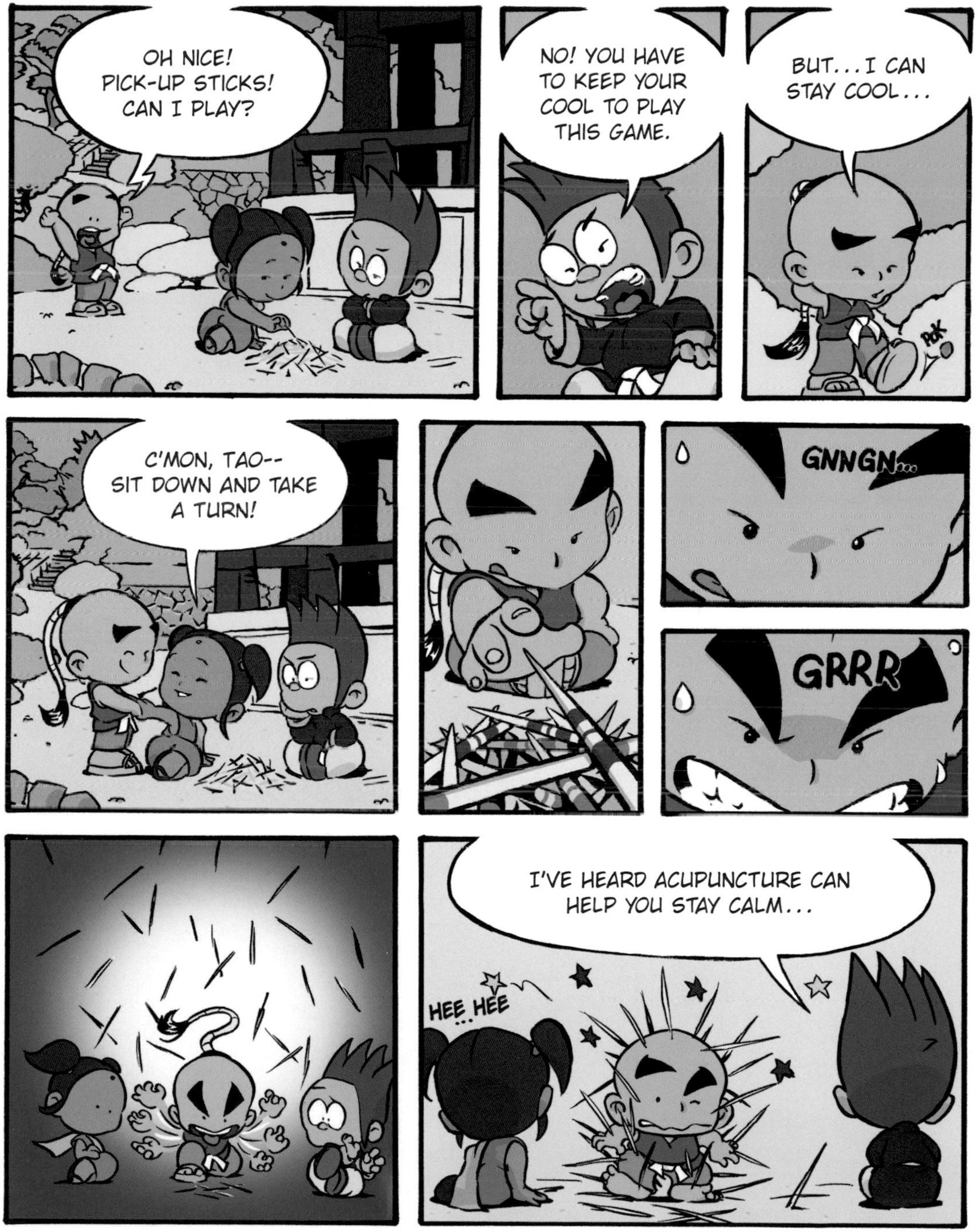
OH NICE! PICK-UP STICKS! CAN I PLAY?
NO! YOU HAVE TO KEEP YOUR COOL TO PLAY THIS GAME.
BUT... I CAN STAY COOL...
POK
C'MON, TAO-- SIT DOWN AND TAKE A TURN!
GNNGN...
GRRR
I'VE HEARD ACUPUNCTURE CAN HELP YOU STAY CALM...
HEE HEE...

A Bird in the Fist

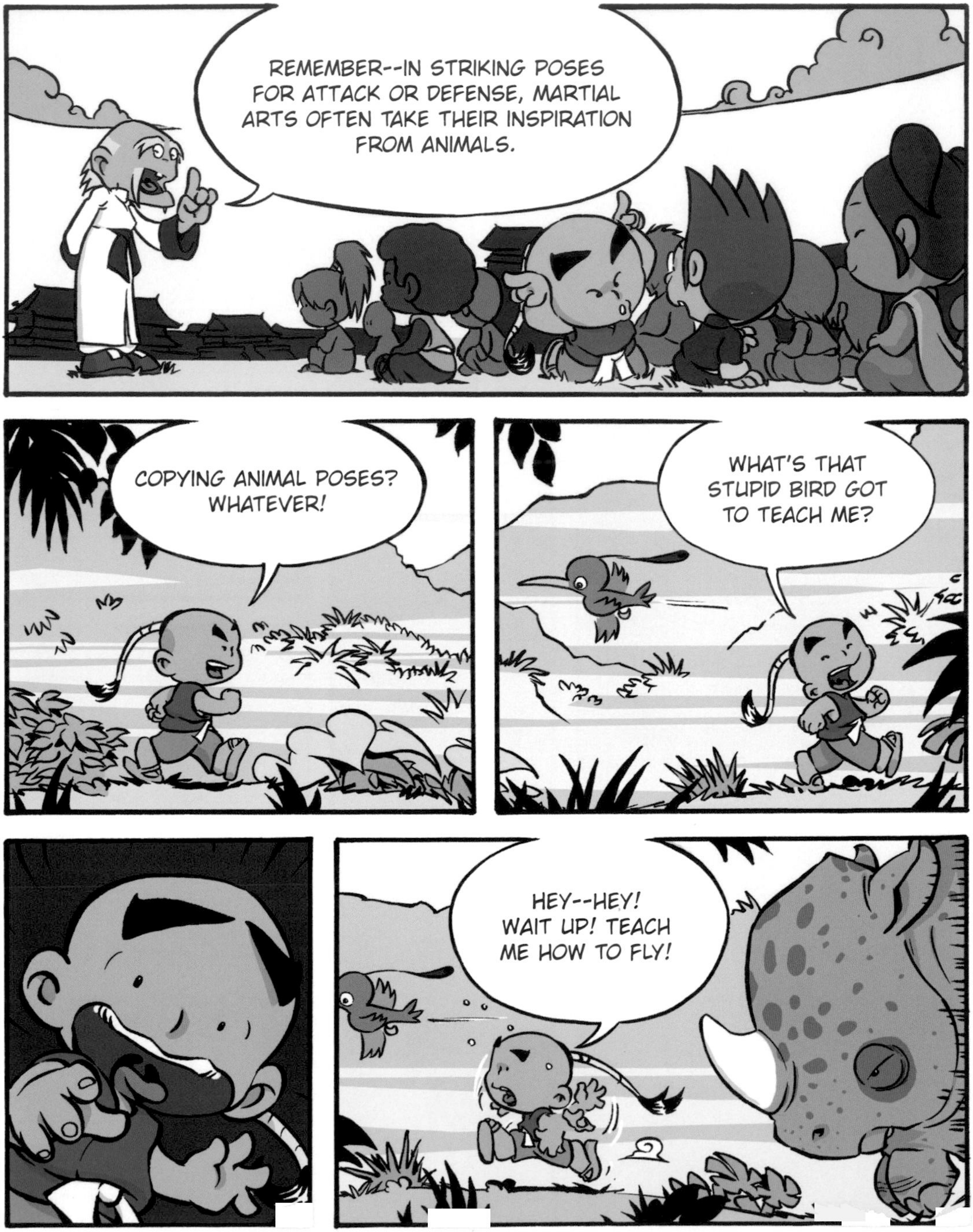

REMEMBER--IN STRIKING POSES FOR ATTACK OR DEFENSE, MARTIAL ARTS OFTEN TAKE THEIR INSPIRATION FROM ANIMALS.
COPYING ANIMAL POSES? WHATEVER!
WHAT'S THAT STUPID BIRD GOT TO TEACH ME?
HEY--HEY! WAIT UP! TEACH ME HOW TO FLY!

Snack Attack

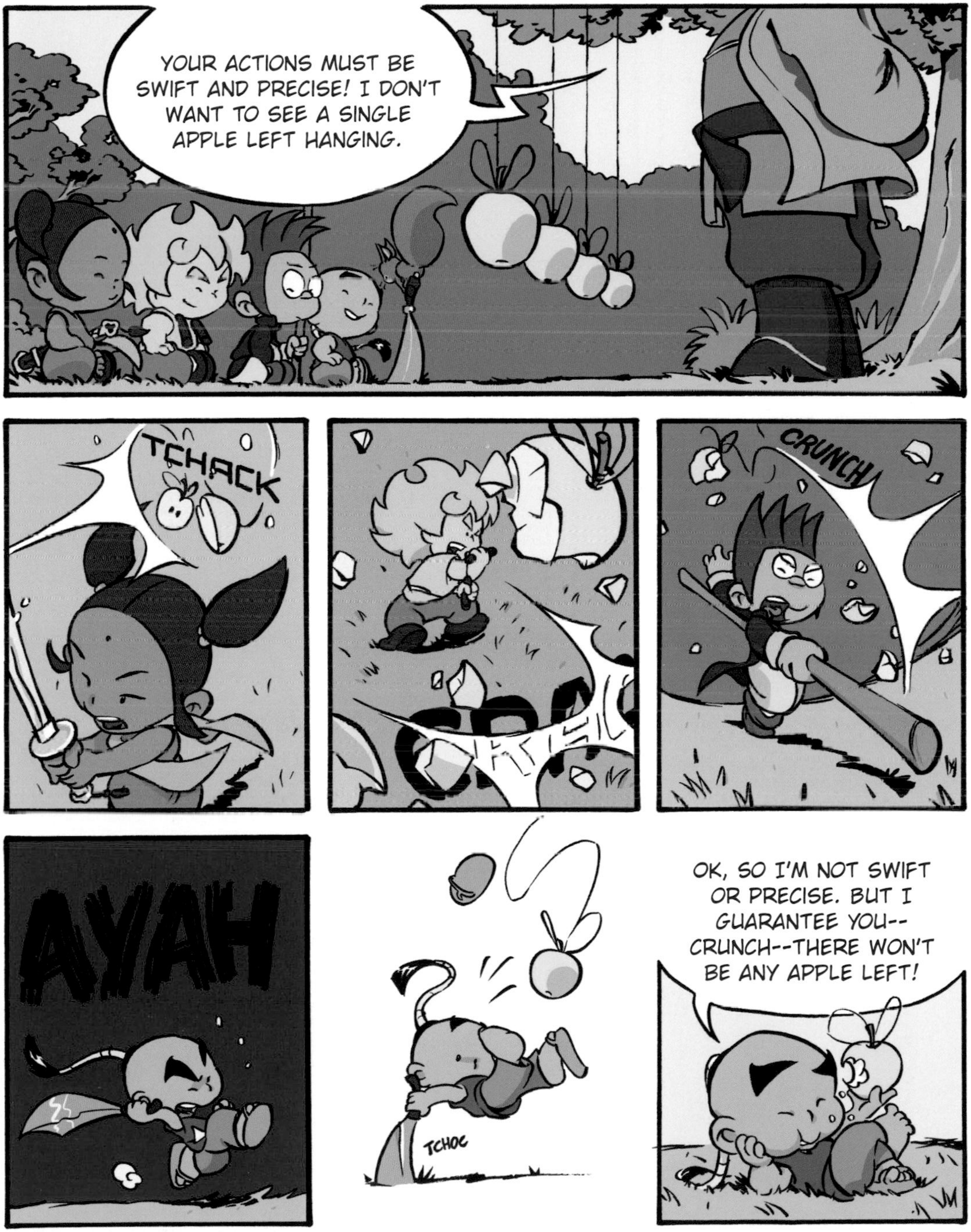
YOUR ACTIONS MUST BE SWIFT AND PRECISE! I DON'T WANT TO SEE A SINGLE APPLE LEFT HANGING.
TCHACK
CRUNCH
AYAH
TCHOC
OK, SO I'M NOT SWIFT OR PRECISE. BUT I GUARANTEE YOU--CRUNCH--THERE WON'T BE ANY APPLE LEFT!

Do unto Your Neighbor's Target

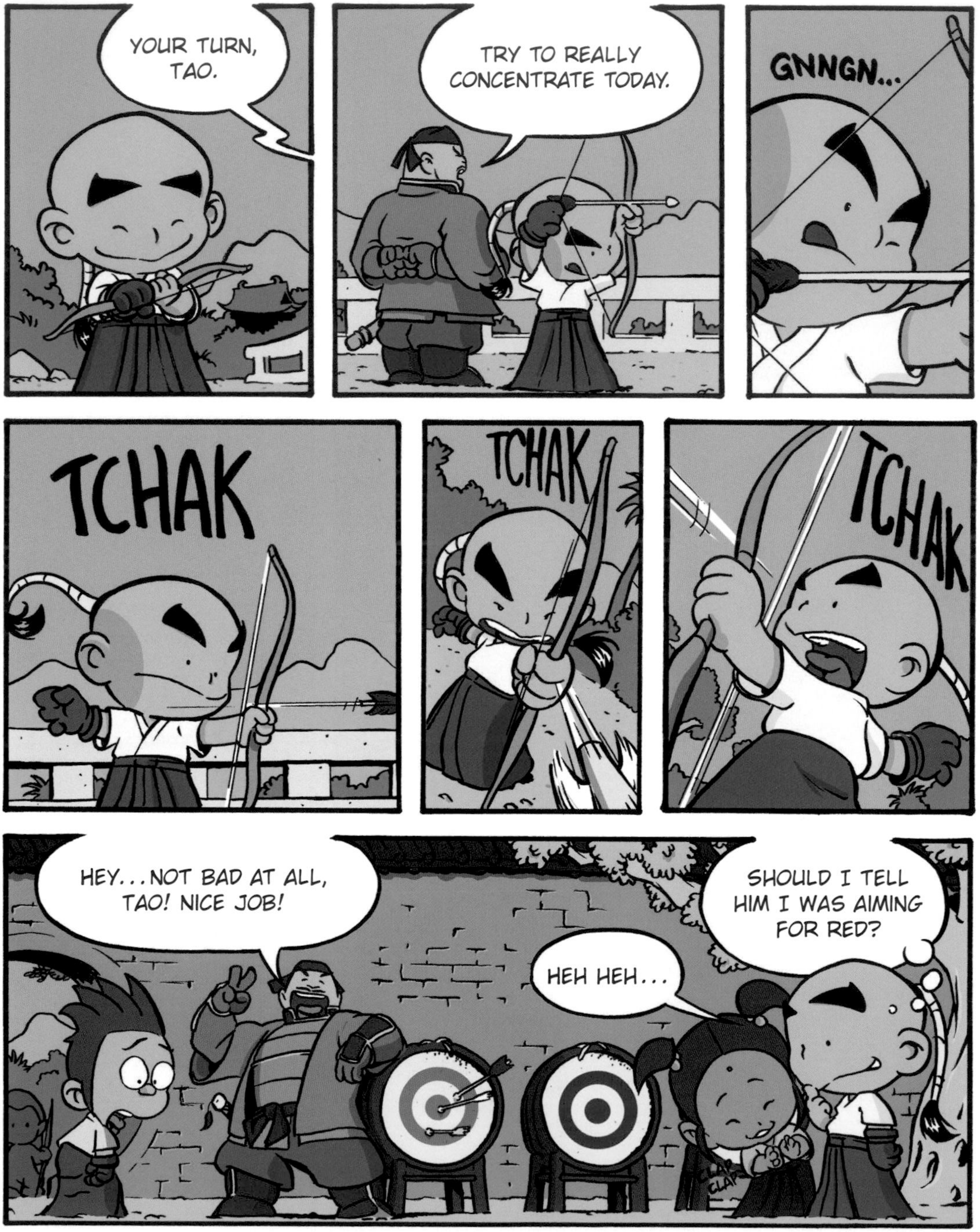

YOUR TURN, TAO.
TRY TO REALLY CONCENTRATE TODAY.
GNNGN...
TCHAK
TCHAK
TCHAK
HEY...NOT BAD AT ALL, TAO! NICE JOB!
HEH HEH...
SHOULD I TELL HIM I WAS AIMING FOR RED?

He Who Spies Gets a Black Eye

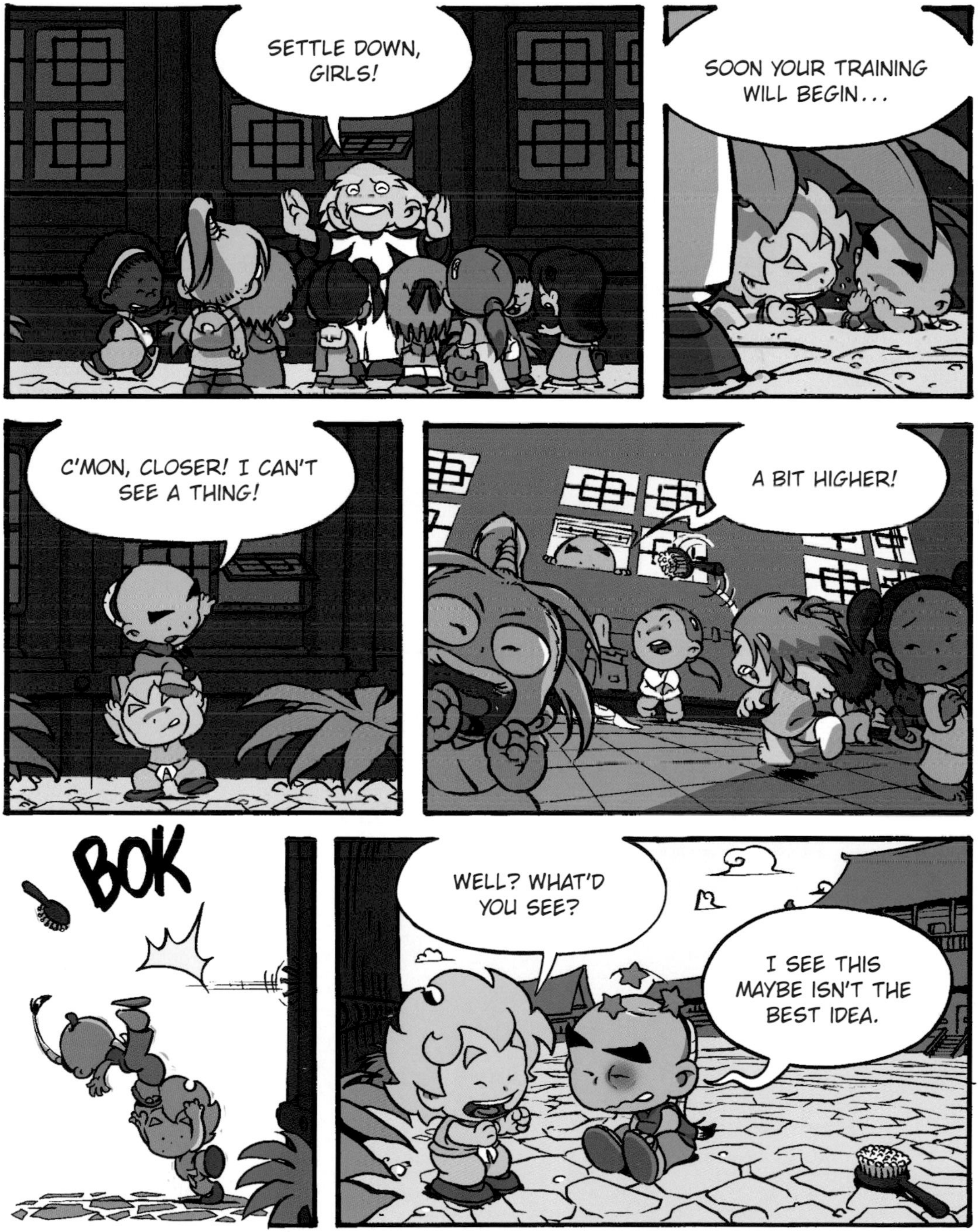
SETTLE DOWN, GIRLS!
SOON YOUR TRAINING WILL BEGIN...
C'MON, CLOSER! I CAN'T SEE A THING!
A BIT HIGHER!
BOK
WELL? WHAT'D YOU SEE?
I SEE THIS MAYBE ISN'T THE BEST IDEA.

The Enemy Within

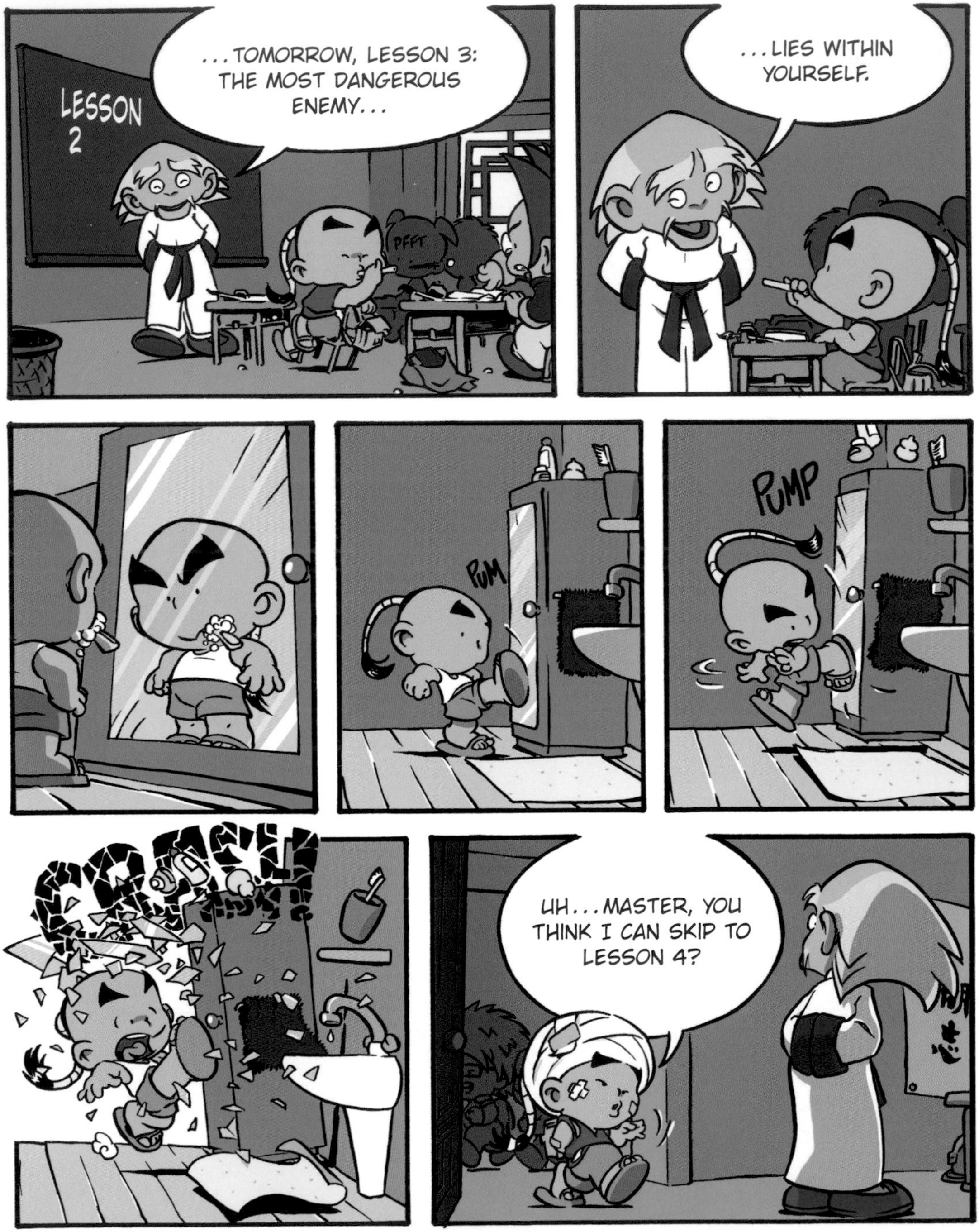

LESSON 2
...TOMORROW, LESSON 3: THE MOST DANGEROUS ENEMY...
PFFT
...LIES WITHIN YOURSELF.
PUM
PUMP
CRASH!
UH...MASTER, YOU THINK I CAN SKIP TO LESSON 4?

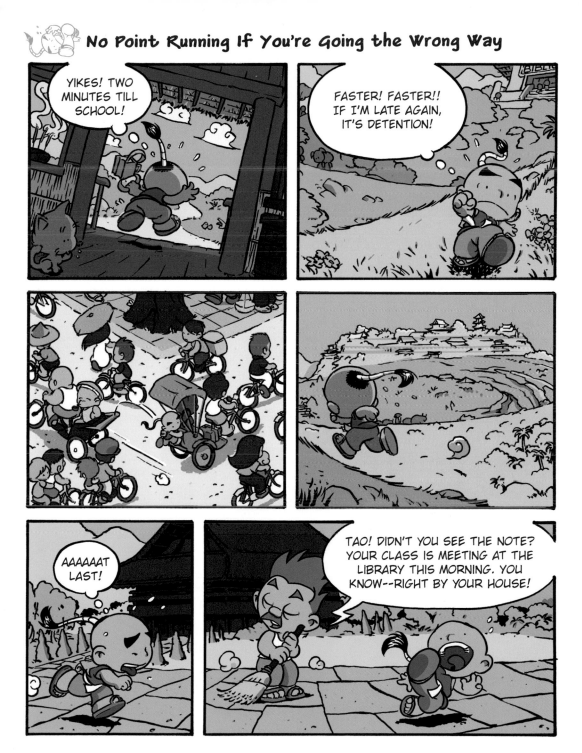

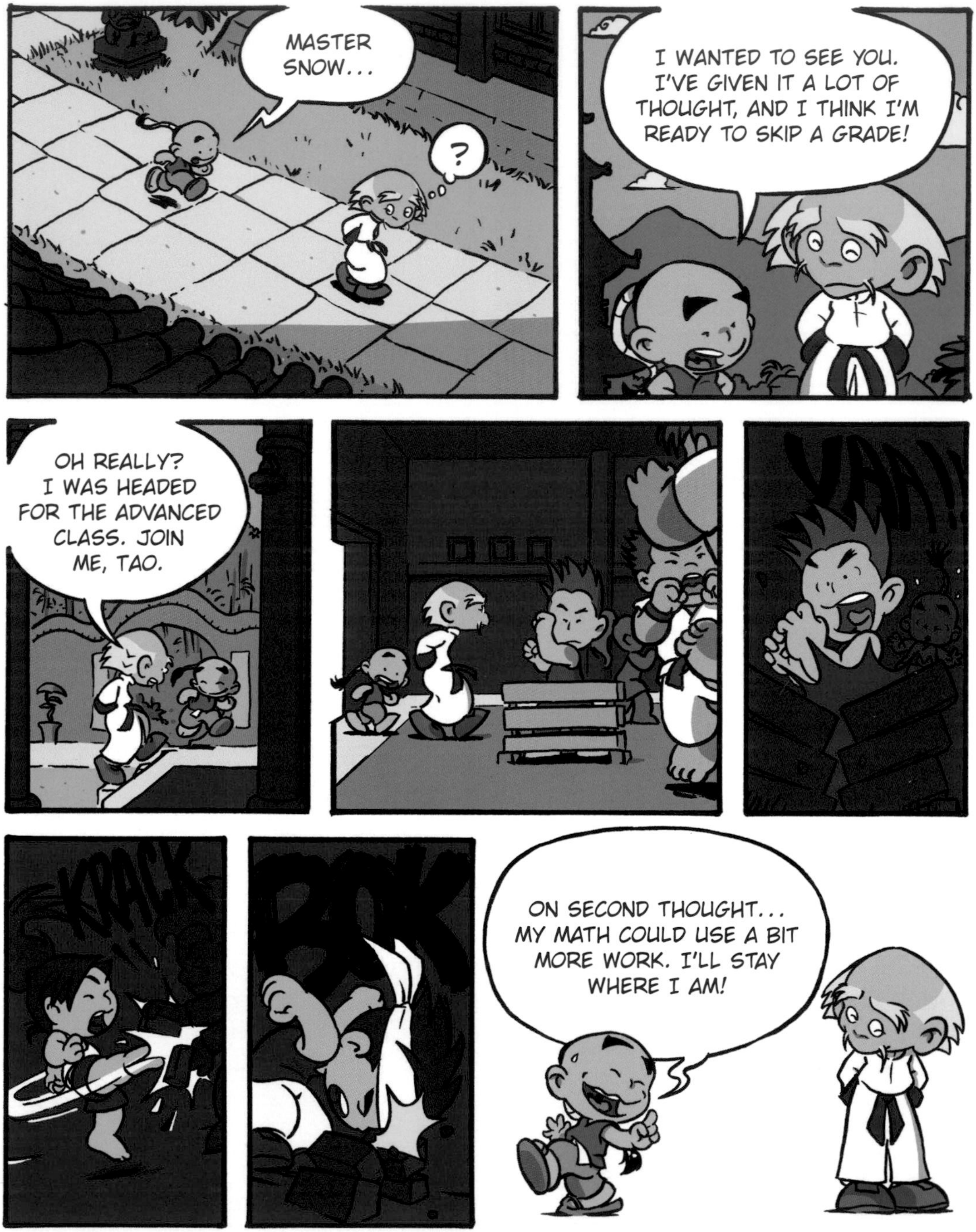
MASTER SNOW...
?
I WANTED TO SEE YOU. I'VE GIVEN IT A LOT OF THOUGHT, AND I THINK I'M READY TO SKIP A GRADE!
OH REALLY? I WAS HEADED FOR THE ADVANCED CLASS. JOIN ME, TAO.
YAH!!
KRACK
BOK
ON SECOND THOUGHT... MY MATH COULD USE A BIT MORE WORK. I'LL STAY WHERE I AM!

YOU'VE GOOFED OFF ALL MORNING, TAO. NOW LOOK DEEP INSIDE YOURSELF FOR SOME MOTIVATION. THEN GET THROUGH THESE OBSTACLES!

READY... SET... GO!

GNNGNNARR...

GONG

LUUUUNCH!

LUNCH???

COMIIIIIINNG!

19

The Joystick Is Mightier than the Sword

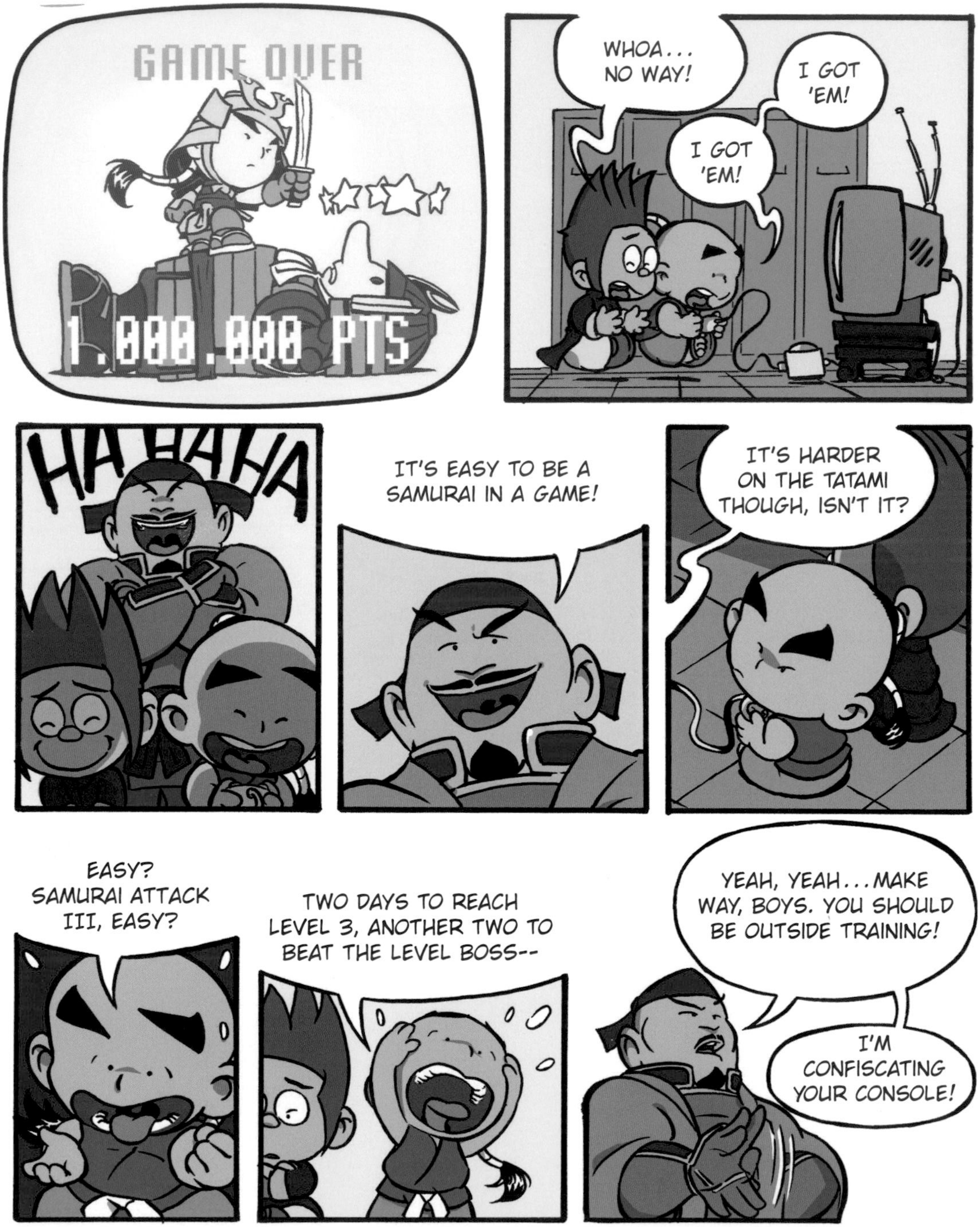
GAME OVER
1.000.000 PTS
WHOA... NO WAY!
I GOT 'EM!
I GOT 'EM!
HA HAHA
IT'S EASY TO BE A SAMURAI IN A GAME!
IT'S HARDER ON THE TATAMI THOUGH, ISN'T IT?
EASY? SAMURAI ATTACK III, EASY?
TWO DAYS TO REACH LEVEL 3, ANOTHER TWO TO BEAT THE LEVEL BOSS--
YEAH, YEAH...MAKE WAY, BOYS. YOU SHOULD BE OUTSIDE TRAINING!
I'M CONFISCATING YOUR CONSOLE!

The Next Day...

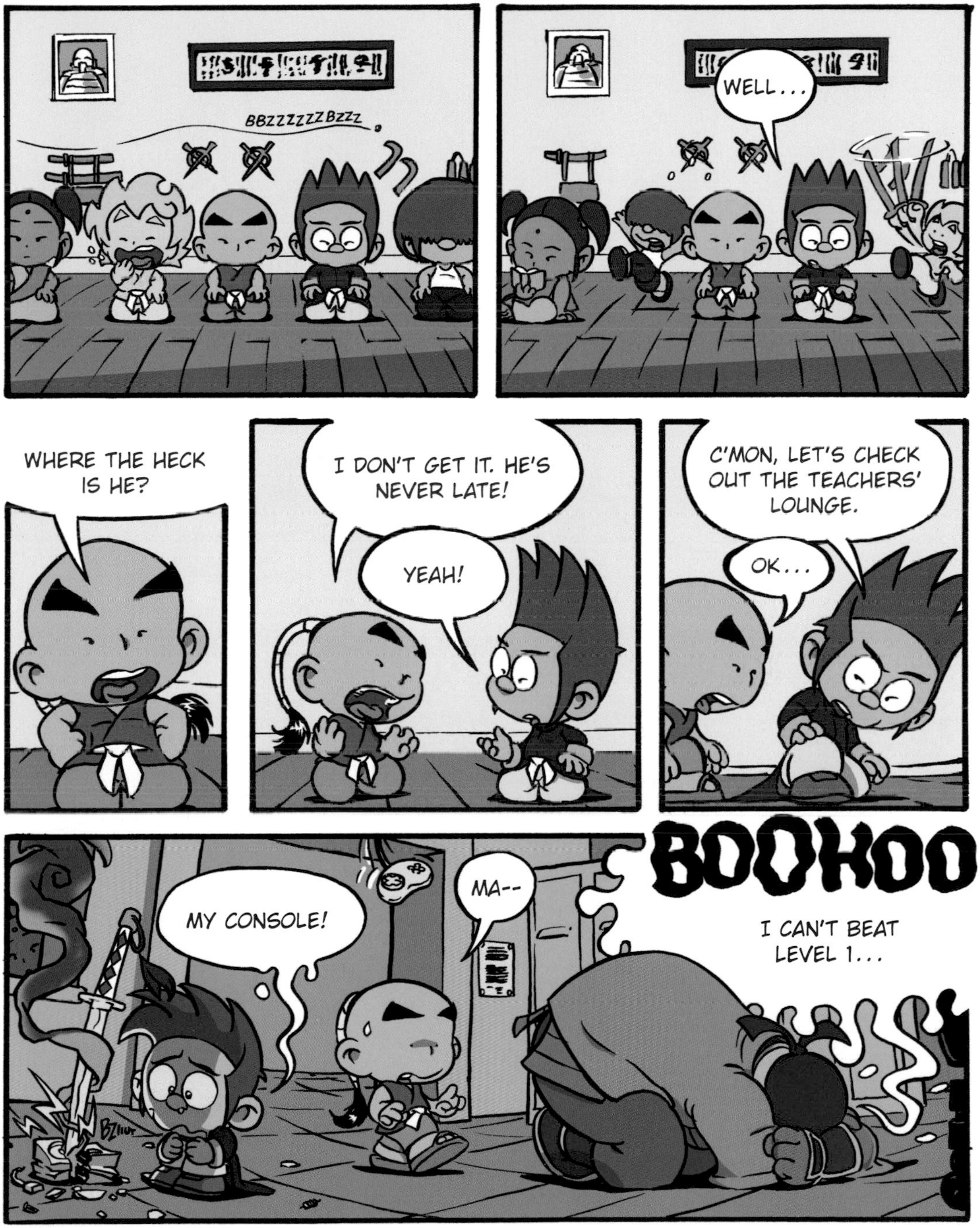
BBZZZZZZBZZZ
WELL...
WHERE THE HECK IS HE?
I DON'T GET IT. HE'S NEVER LATE!
YEAH!
C'MON, LET'S CHECK OUT THE TEACHERS' LOUNGE.
OK...
BOOHOO
MY CONSOLE!
MA--
I CAN'T BEAT LEVEL 1...

Wise Men Waste No Words

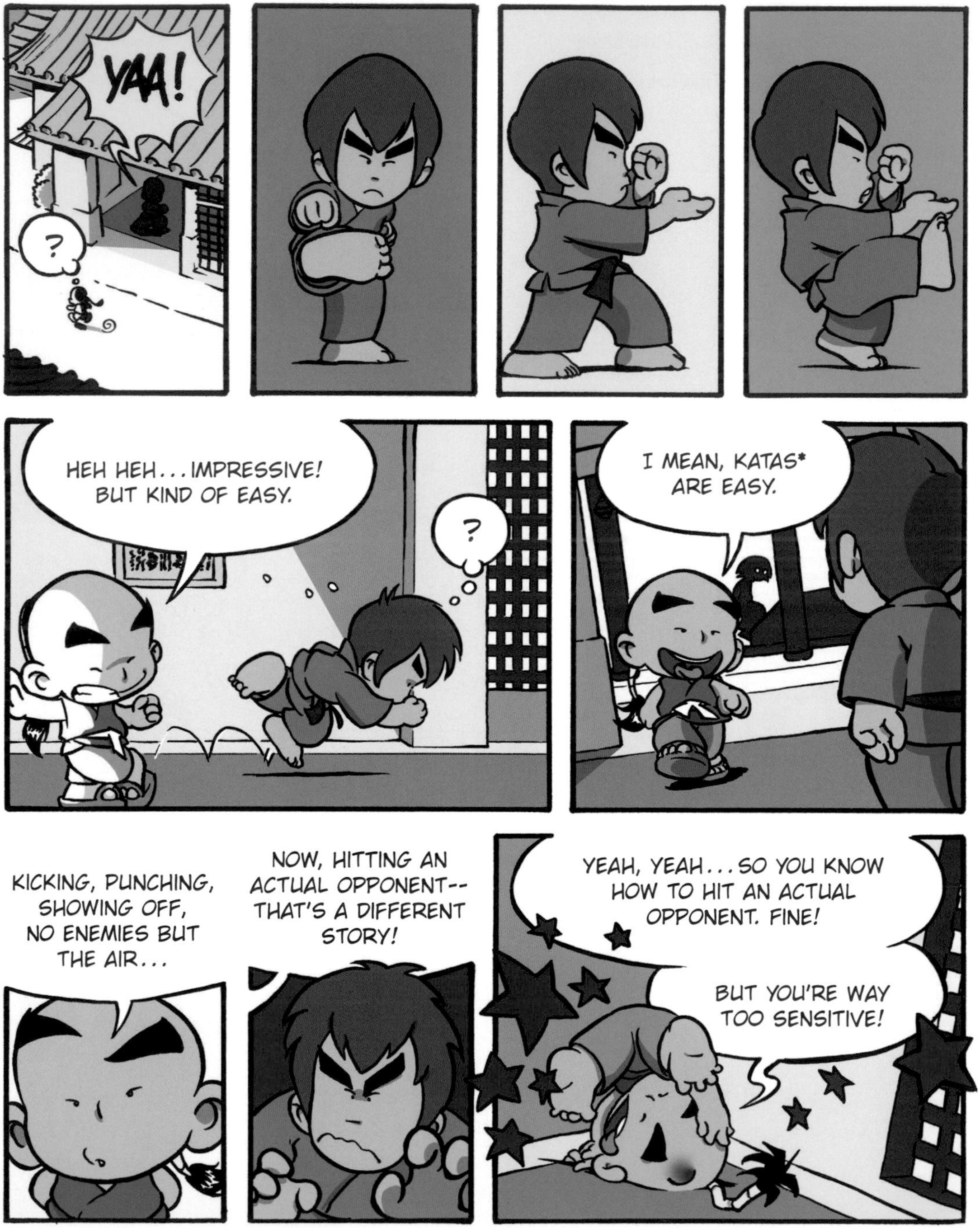
YAA!
?
HEH HEH . . . IMPRESSIVE! BUT KIND OF EASY.
?
I MEAN, KATAS* ARE EASY.
KICKING, PUNCHING, SHOWING OFF, NO ENEMIES BUT THE AIR . . .
NOW, HITTING AN ACTUAL OPPONENT-- THAT'S A DIFFERENT STORY!
YEAH, YEAH . . . SO YOU KNOW HOW TO HIT AN ACTUAL OPPONENT. FINE!
BUT YOU'RE WAY TOO SENSITIVE!

*KATA: JAPANESE WORD FOR CHOREOGRAPHED PATTERNS OF MARTIAL ARTS MOVEMENT

A Chirping Grasshopper Makes for Noisy Silence

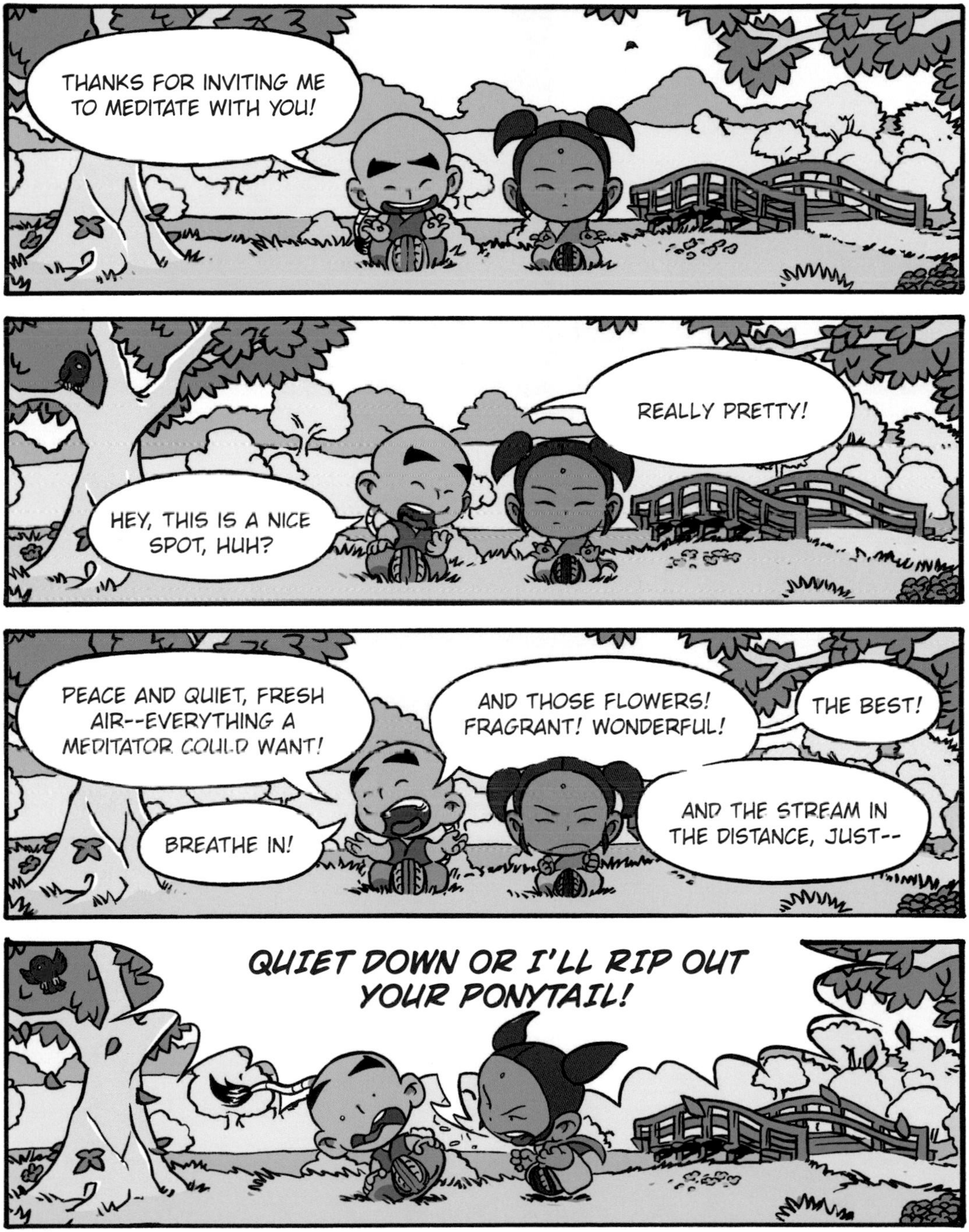
THANKS FOR INVITING ME TO MEDITATE WITH YOU!
HEY, THIS IS A NICE SPOT, HUH?
REALLY PRETTY!
PEACE AND QUIET, FRESH AIR--EVERYTHING A MEDITATOR COULD WANT!
BREATHE IN!
AND THOSE FLOWERS! FRAGRANT! WONDERFUL!
THE BEST!
AND THE STREAM IN THE DISTANCE, JUST--
QUIET DOWN OR I'LL RIP OUT YOUR PONYTAIL!

Reading Can Prevent Kata-strophe

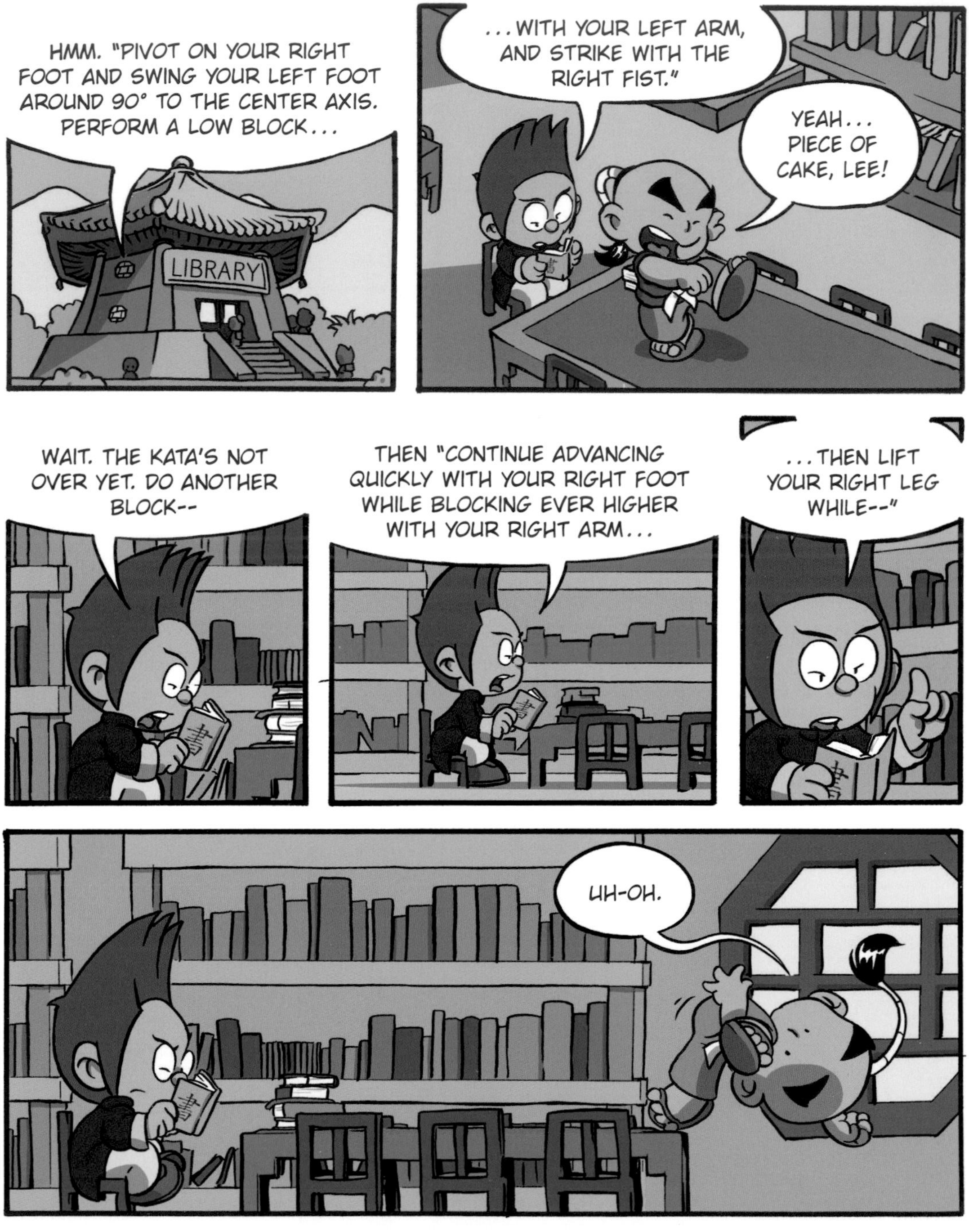
HMM. "PIVOT ON YOUR RIGHT FOOT AND SWING YOUR LEFT FOOT AROUND 90° TO THE CENTER AXIS. PERFORM A LOW BLOCK...
LIBRARY
...WITH YOUR LEFT ARM, AND STRIKE WITH THE RIGHT FIST."
YEAH... PIECE OF CAKE, LEE!
WAIT. THE KATA'S NOT OVER YET. DO ANOTHER BLOCK--
THEN "CONTINUE ADVANCING QUICKLY WITH YOUR RIGHT FOOT WHILE BLOCKING EVER HIGHER WITH YOUR RIGHT ARM...
...THEN LIFT YOUR RIGHT LEG WHILE--"
UH-OH.

The Great Dragon Eats the Tiny Boat

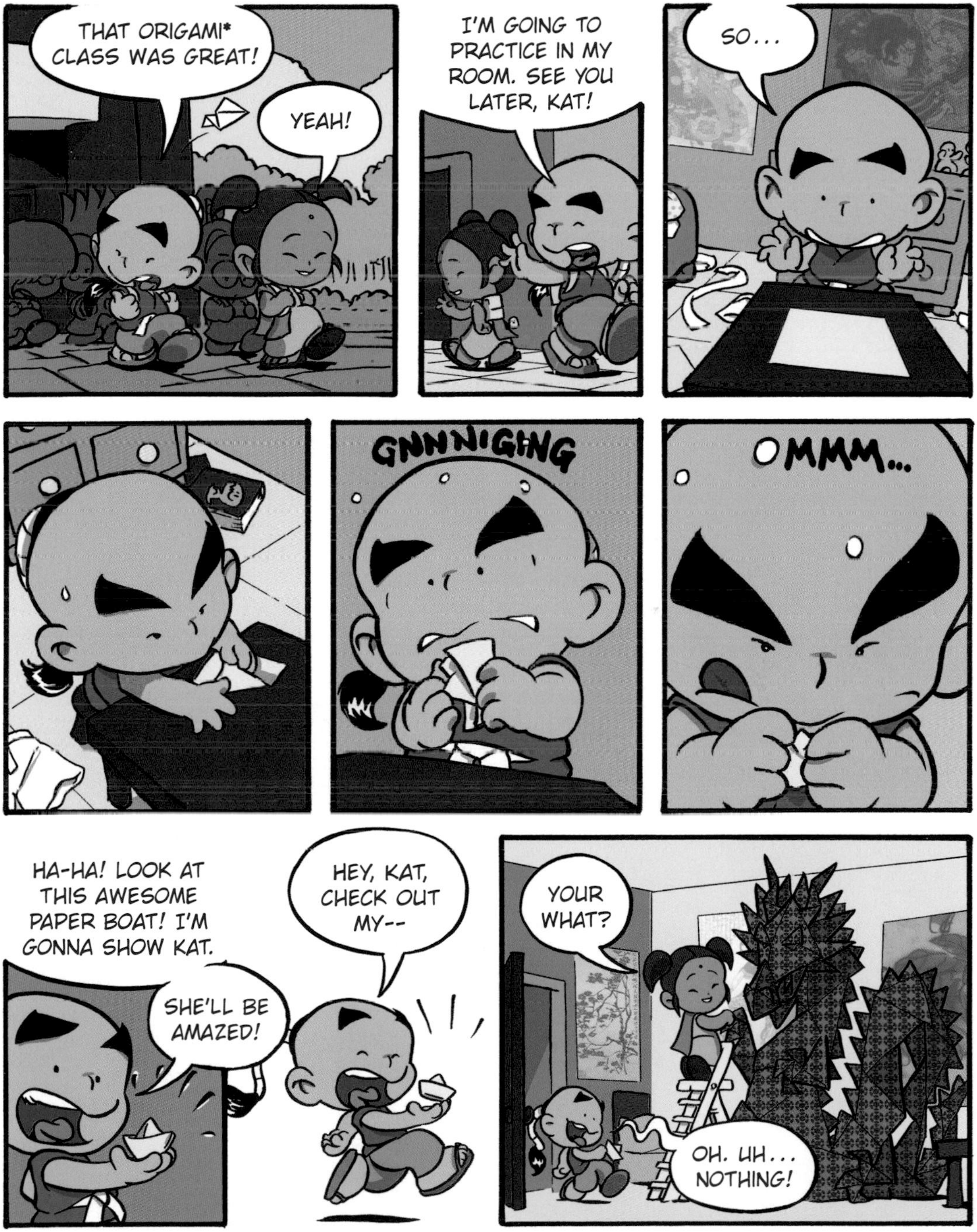
THAT ORIGAMI* CLASS WAS GREAT!
YEAH!
I'M GOING TO PRACTICE IN MY ROOM. SEE YOU LATER, KAT!
SO...
GNNNIGING
OMMM...
HA-HA! LOOK AT THIS AWESOME PAPER BOAT! I'M GONNA SHOW KAT.
SHE'LL BE AMAZED!
HEY, KAT, CHECK OUT MY--
YOUR WHAT?
OH. UH... NOTHING!

*ORIGAMI: THE JAPANESE ART OF PAPER FOLDING

Soul of a Poet, Belly of a Hungry Man

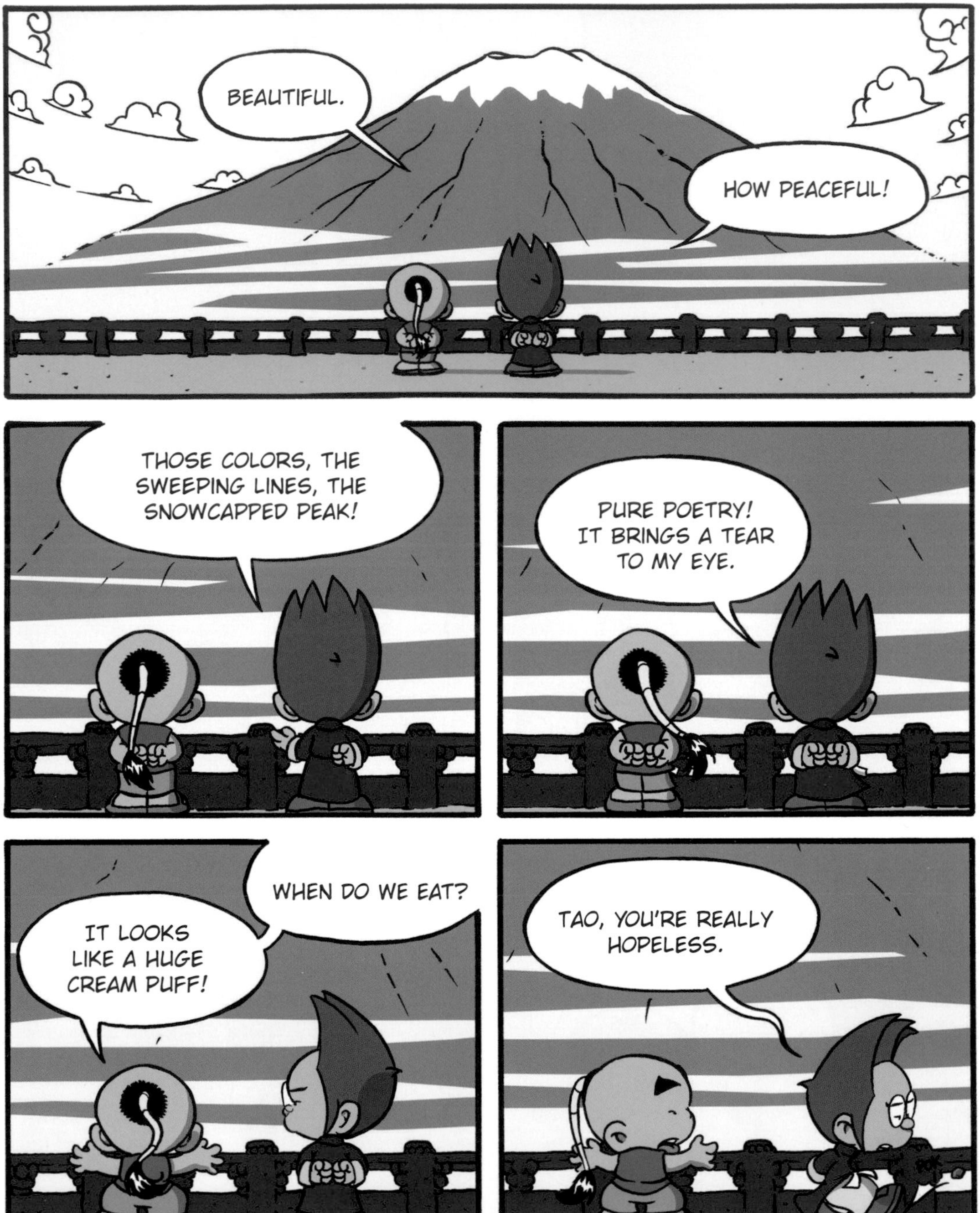

BEAUTIFUL.
HOW PEACEFUL!
THOSE COLORS, THE SWEEPING LINES, THE SNOWCAPPED PEAK!
PURE POETRY! IT BRINGS A TEAR TO MY EYE.
IT LOOKS LIKE A HUGE CREAM PUFF!
WHEN DO WE EAT?
TAO, YOU'RE REALLY HOPELESS.

The Horror, the Horror

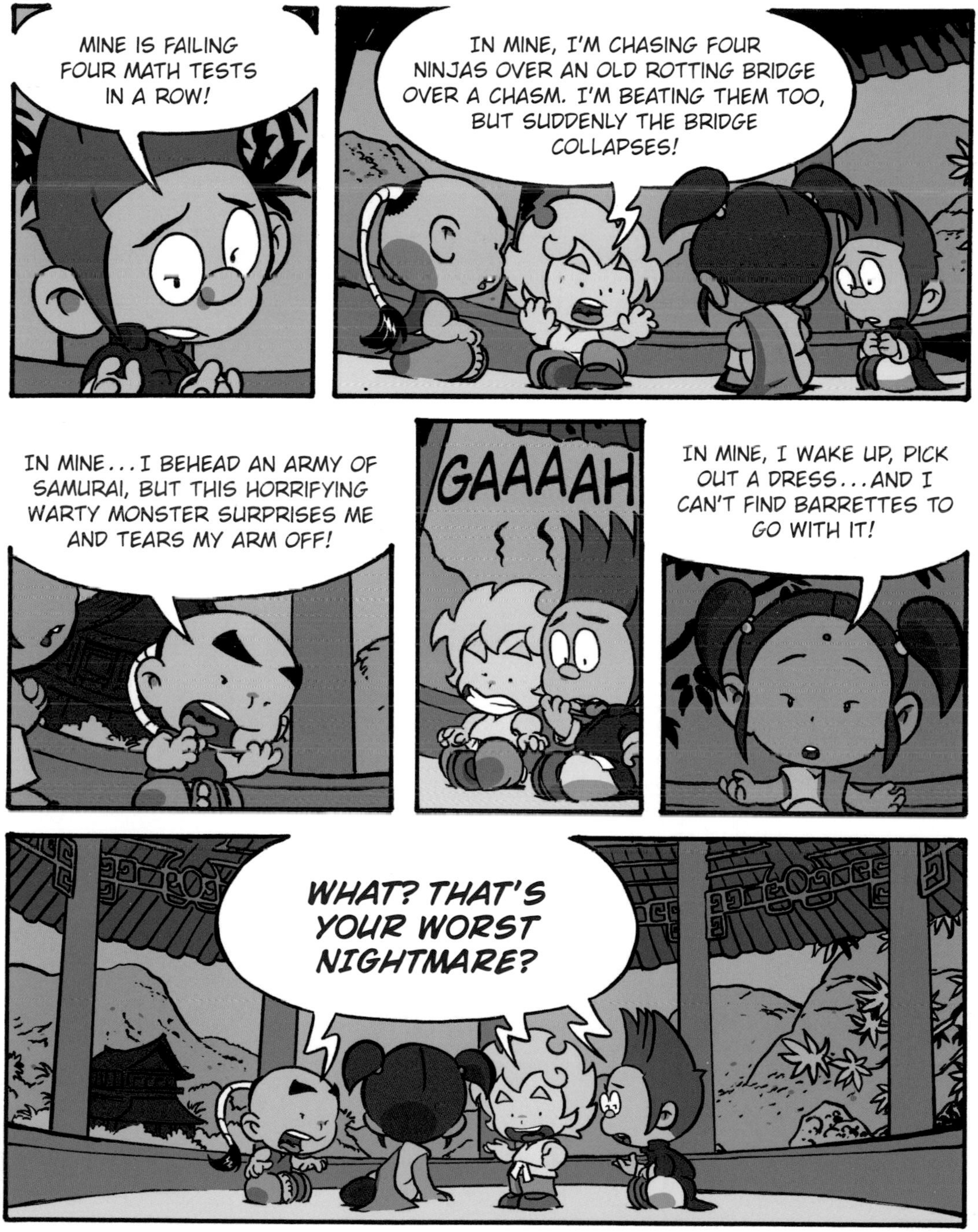
MINE IS FAILING FOUR MATH TESTS IN A ROW!
IN MINE, I'M CHASING FOUR NINJAS OVER AN OLD ROTTING BRIDGE OVER A CHASM. I'M BEATING THEM TOO, BUT SUDDENLY THE BRIDGE COLLAPSES!
IN MINE... I BEHEAD AN ARMY OF SAMURAI, BUT THIS HORRIFYING WARTY MONSTER SURPRISES ME AND TEARS MY ARM OFF!
GAAAAH
IN MINE, I WAKE UP, PICK OUT A DRESS... AND I CAN'T FIND BARRETTES TO GO WITH IT!
WHAT? THAT'S YOUR WORST NIGHTMARE?

Good, Clean Fun

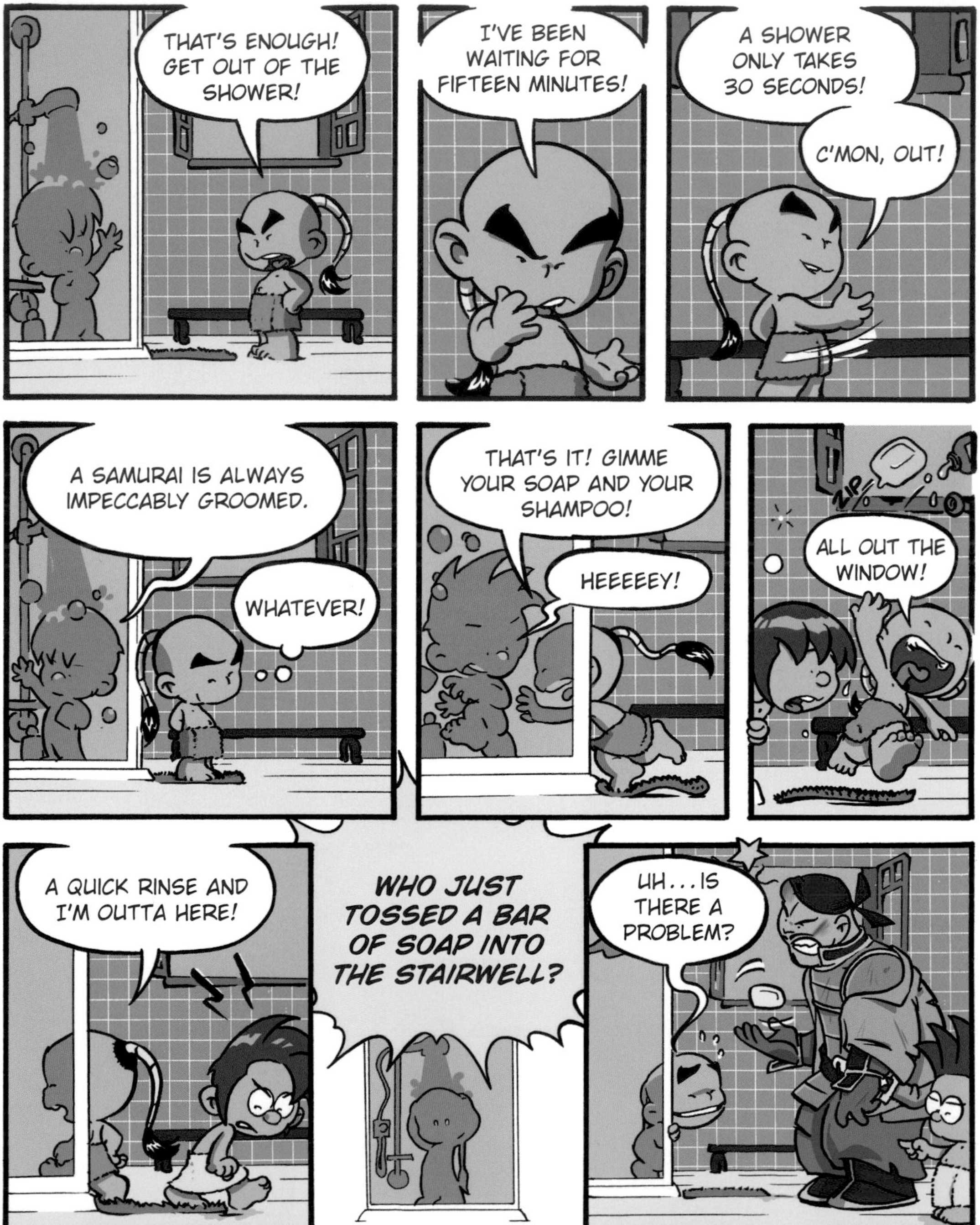

THAT'S ENOUGH! GET OUT OF THE SHOWER!
I'VE BEEN WAITING FOR FIFTEEN MINUTES!
A SHOWER ONLY TAKES 30 SECONDS!
C'MON, OUT!
A SAMURAI IS ALWAYS IMPECCABLY GROOMED.
WHATEVER!
THAT'S IT! GIMME YOUR SOAP AND YOUR SHAMPOO!
HEEEEEY!
ZIP
ALL OUT THE WINDOW!
A QUICK RINSE AND I'M OUTTA HERE!
WHO JUST TOSSED A BAR OF SOAP INTO THE STAIRWELL?
UH...IS THERE A PROBLEM?

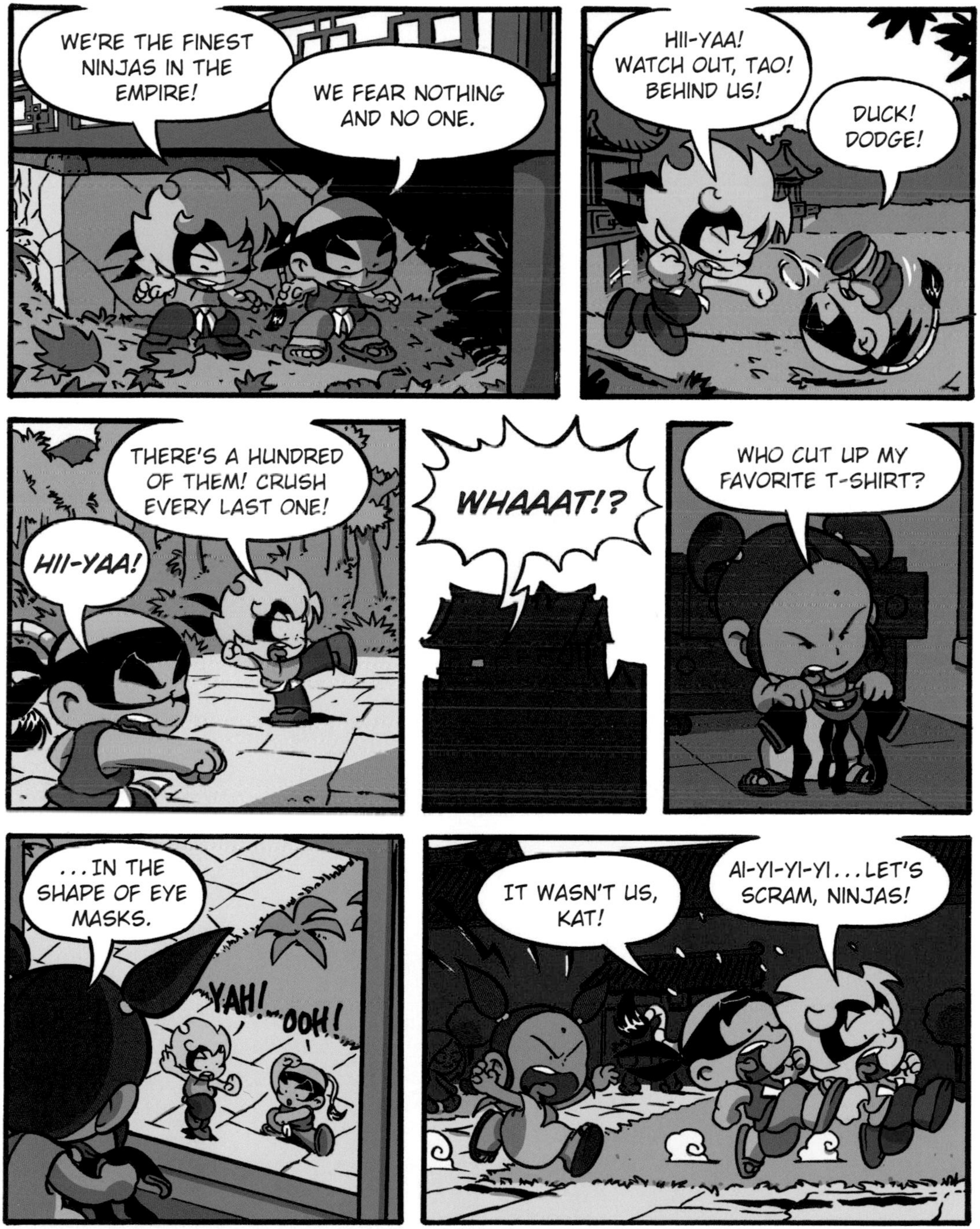
WE'RE THE FINEST NINJAS IN THE EMPIRE!
WE FEAR NOTHING AND NO ONE.
HII-YAA! WATCH OUT, TAO! BEHIND US!
DUCK! DODGE!
THERE'S A HUNDRED OF THEM! CRUSH EVERY LAST ONE!
HII-YAA!
WHAAAT!?
WHO CUT UP MY FAVORITE T-SHIRT?
...IN THE SHAPE OF EYE MASKS.
YAH!
OOH!
IT WASN'T US, KAT!
AI-YI-YI-YI...LET'S SCRAM, NINJAS!

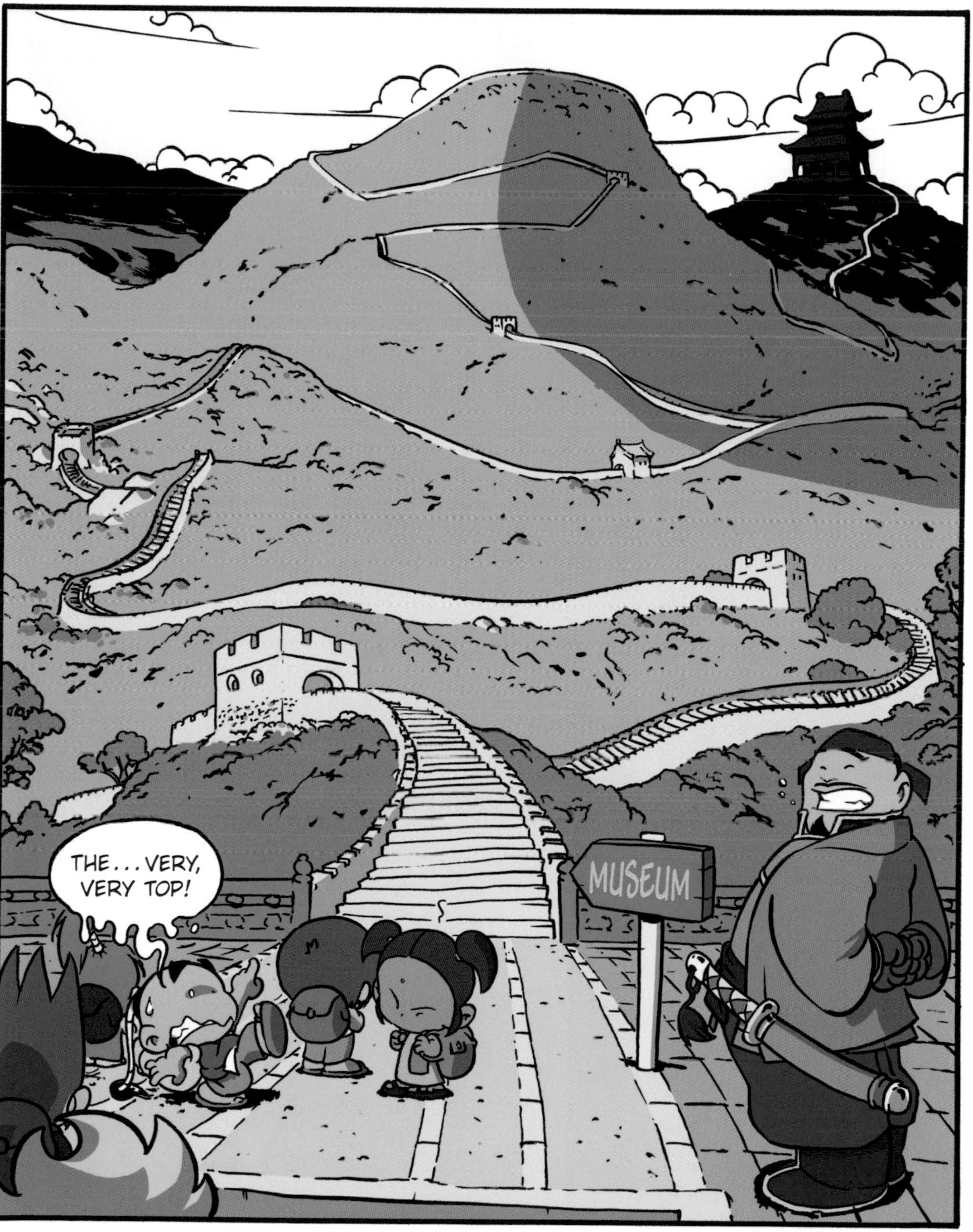
THE...VERY, VERY TOP!
MUSEUM

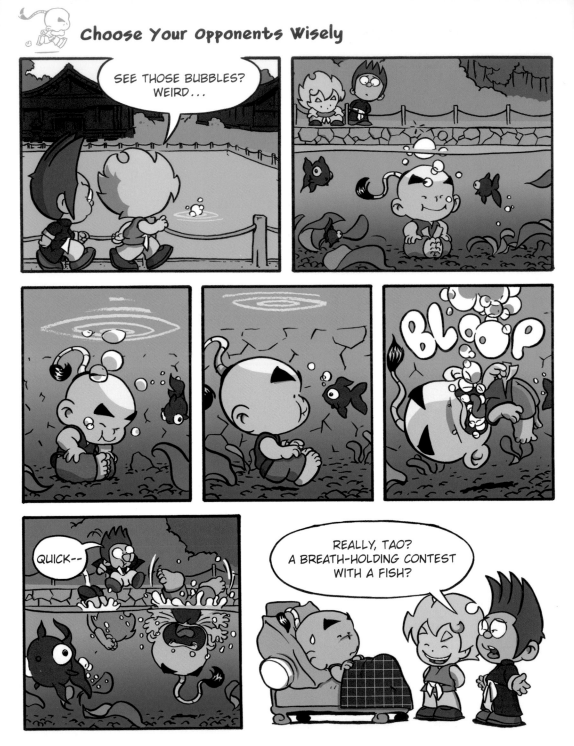

A Grandmaster Has His Secrets

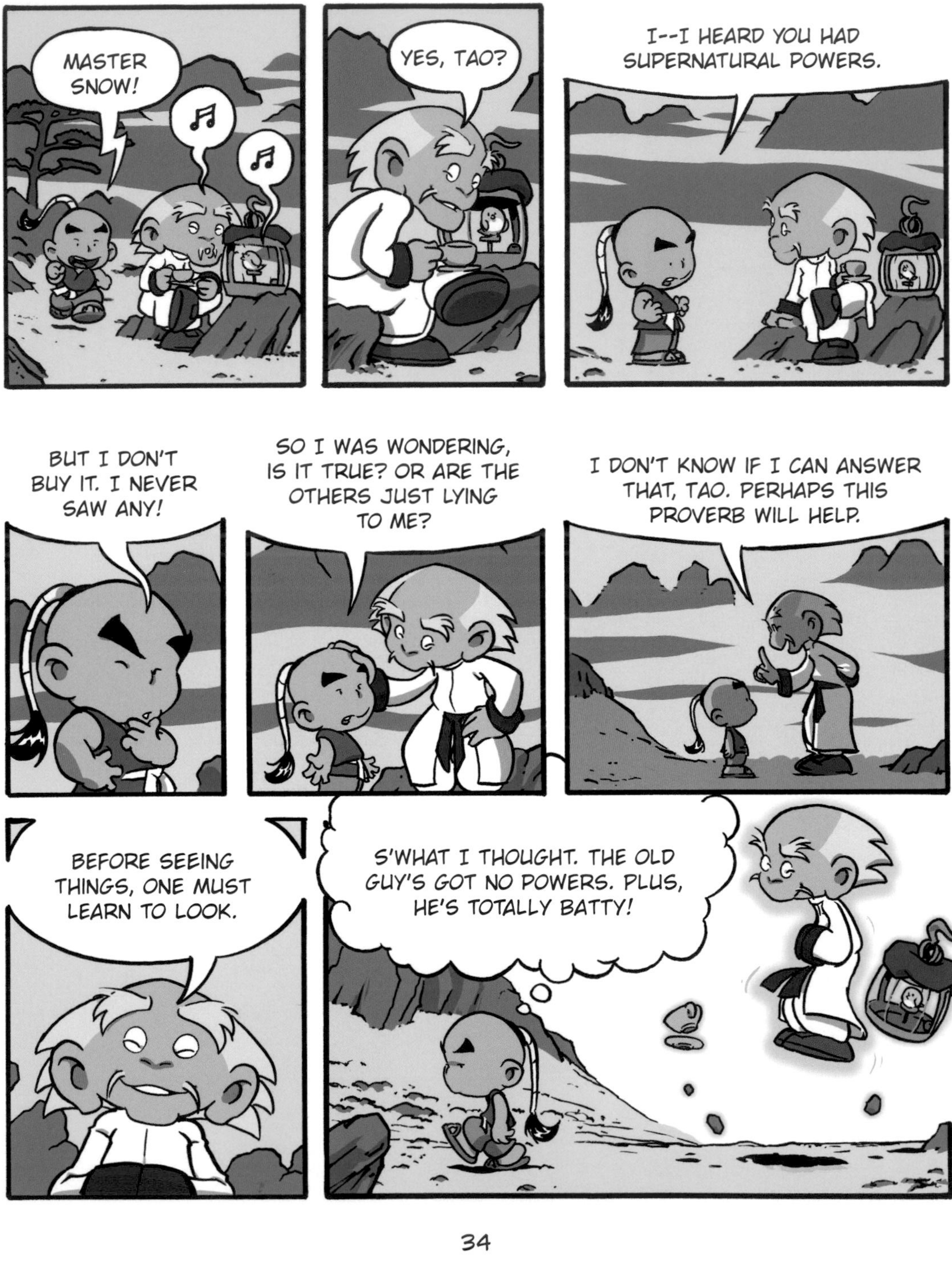
MASTER SNOW!
♫
♫
YES, TAO?
I--I HEARD YOU HAD SUPERNATURAL POWERS.
BUT I DON'T BUY IT. I NEVER SAW ANY!
SO I WAS WONDERING, IS IT TRUE? OR ARE THE OTHERS JUST LYING TO ME?
I DON'T KNOW IF I CAN ANSWER THAT, TAO. PERHAPS THIS PROVERB WILL HELP.
BEFORE SEEING THINGS, ONE MUST LEARN TO LOOK.
S'WHAT I THOUGHT. THE OLD GUY'S GOT NO POWERS. PLUS, HE'S TOTALLY BATTY!

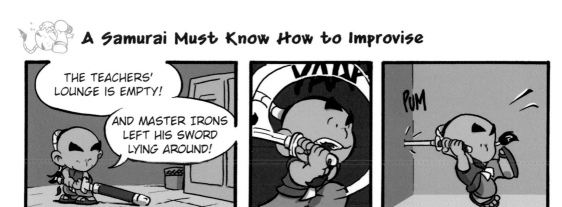

He Who Cannot Fly Must Avoid Falling

The Longest Route Is Not Always the Best

HEY, KID! CAN YOU TELL ME HOW TO GET TO THE BLUE DRAGON DOJO?

UM... TAKE THE BIG PATH THROUGH THE PARK, TURN RIGHT AT THE RED SIGN, AND GO UPSTAIRS.

OK.

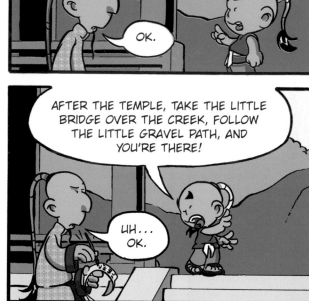

THEN TURN LEFT UP TOP. BLUE DOOR... KEEP GOING FOR THREE MINUTES...

AFTER THE TEMPLE, TAKE THE LITTLE BRIDGE OVER THE CREEK, FOLLOW THE LITTLE GRAVEL PATH, AND YOU'RE THERE!

UH... OK.

SO THEN I'LL BE AT THE BLUE DRAGON DOJO?

NAH! BUT YOU'LL FIND A MAP OF THE SCHOOL!

Missing the Point

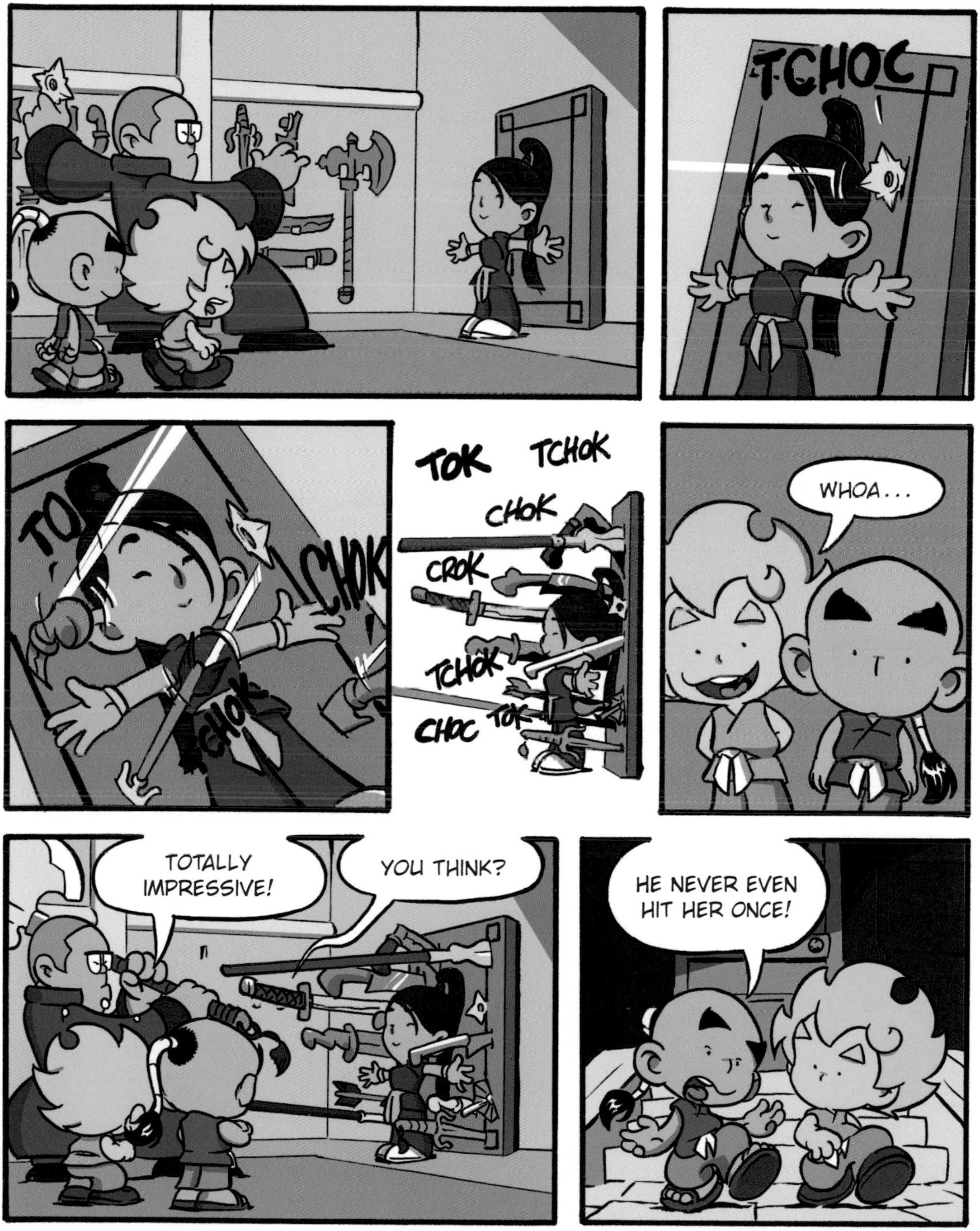

TCHOC
TOP
CHOK
CHOK
TOK
TCHOK
CHOK
CROK
TCHOK
CHOC
TOK
WHOA...
TOTALLY IMPRESSIVE!
YOU THINK?
HE NEVER EVEN HIT HER ONCE!

A Studious Grasshopper Is Never Late

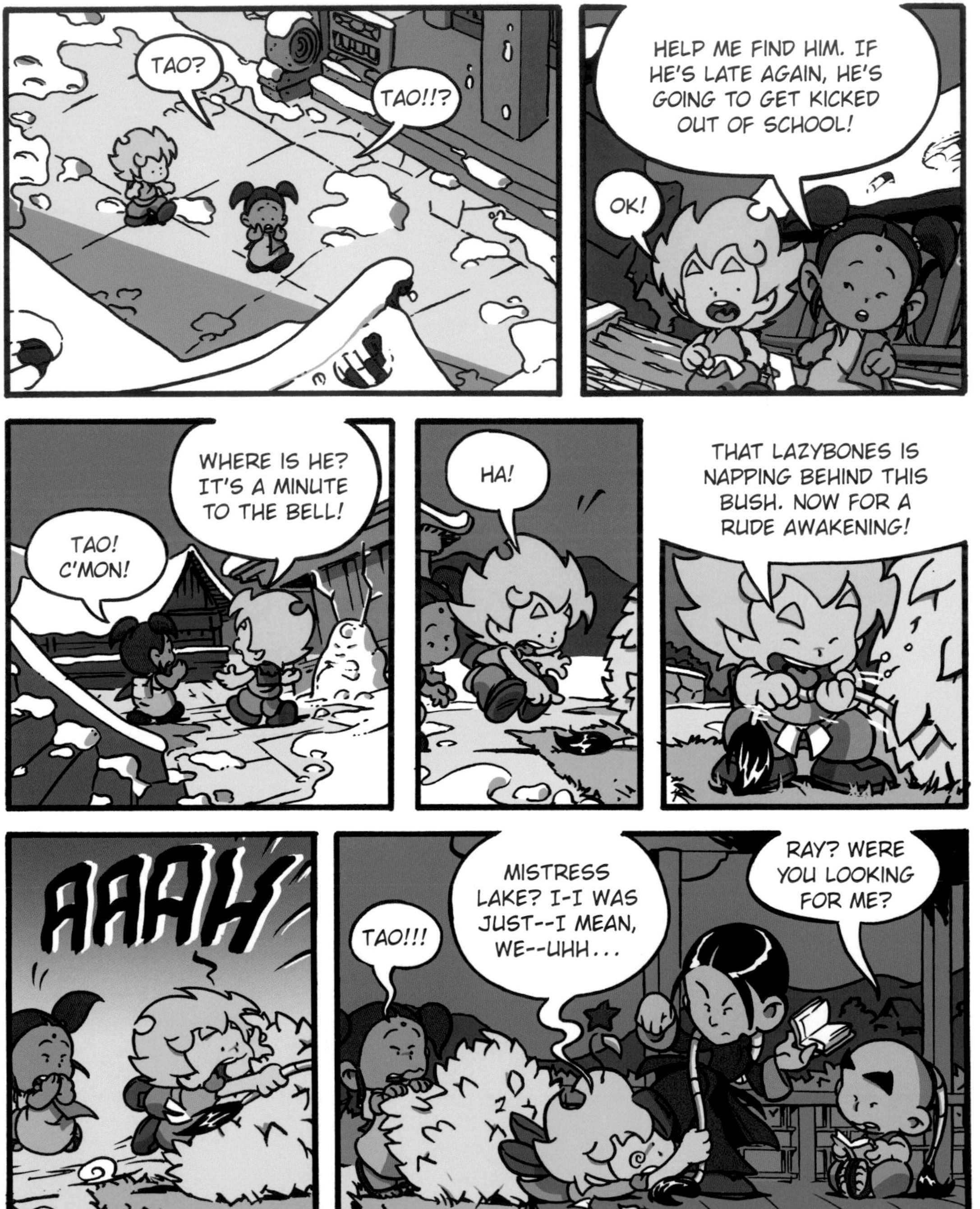
TAO?
TAO!!?
HELP ME FIND HIM. IF HE'S LATE AGAIN, HE'S GOING TO GET KICKED OUT OF SCHOOL!
OK!
WHERE IS HE? IT'S A MINUTE TO THE BELL!
TAO! C'MON!
HA!
THAT LAZYBONES IS NAPPING BEHIND THIS BUSH. NOW FOR A RUDE AWAKENING!
AAAH
TAO!!!
MISTRESS LAKE? I-I WAS JUST--I MEAN, WE--UHH...
RAY? WERE YOU LOOKING FOR ME?

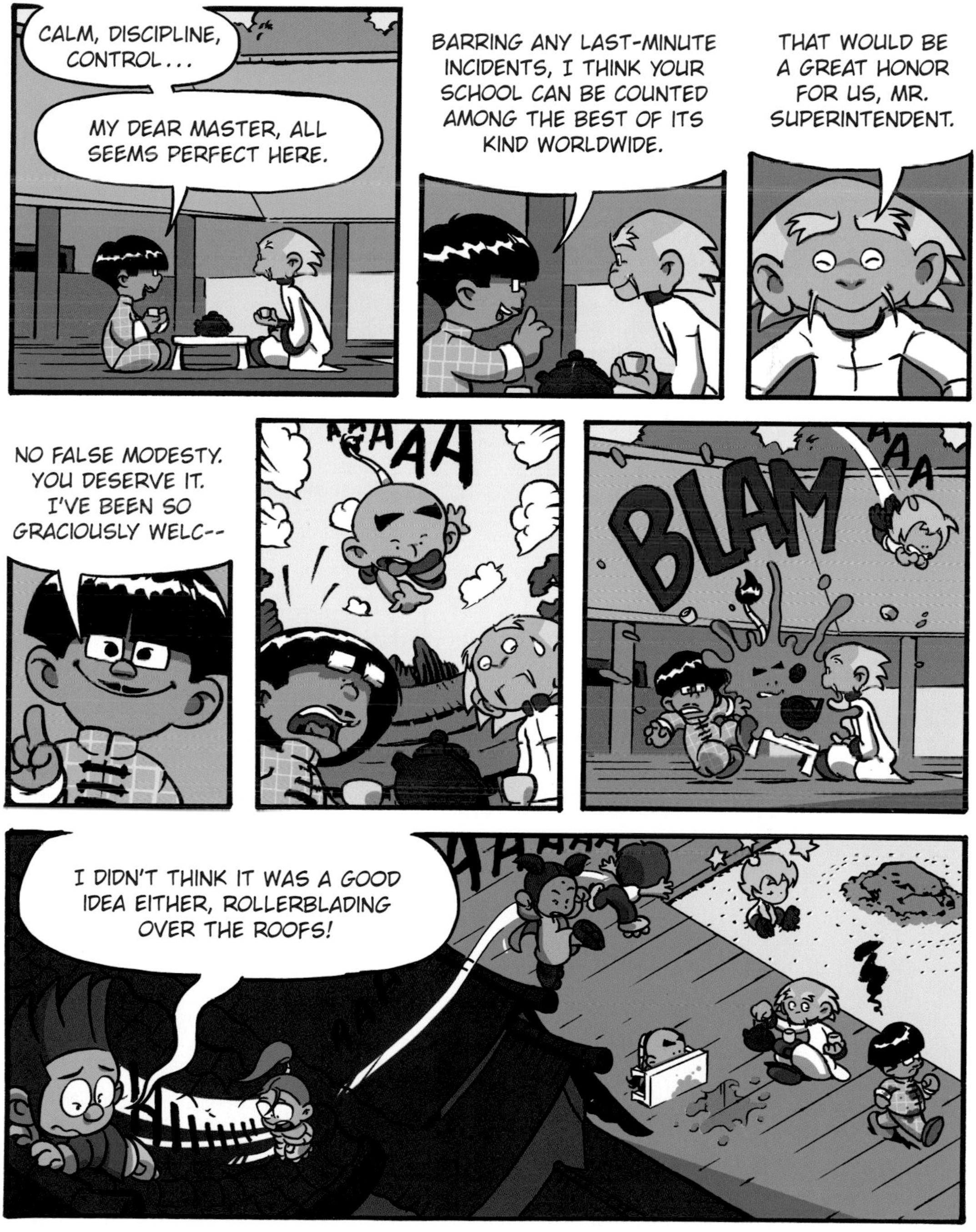
CALM, DISCIPLINE, CONTROL . . .
MY DEAR MASTER, ALL SEEMS PERFECT HERE.
BARRING ANY LAST-MINUTE INCIDENTS, I THINK YOUR SCHOOL CAN BE COUNTED AMONG THE BEST OF ITS KIND WORLDWIDE.
THAT WOULD BE A GREAT HONOR FOR US, MR. SUPERINTENDENT.
NO FALSE MODESTY. YOU DESERVE IT. I'VE BEEN SO GRACIOUSLY WELC--
AAAA
BLAM
AAA
I DIDN'T THINK IT WAS A GOOD IDEA EITHER, ROLLERBLADING OVER THE ROOFS!

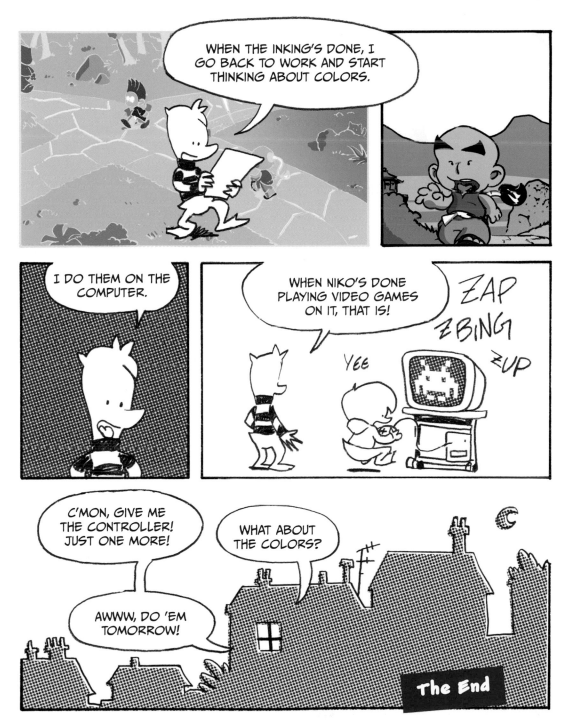

TAO
The Little Samurai